A TASTE OF CHARDONNAY

D0167144

A TASTE OF CHARDONNAY

The Napa Wine Heiresses

Heather Heyford

eKENSINGTON BOOKS
KENSINGTON PUBLISHING CORP.
www.kensingtonbooks.com

eKENSINGTON BOOKS are published by

Kensington Publishing Corp.
119 West 40th Street
New York, NY 10018

All Kensington titles, imprints, and distributed lines are available at special quantity discounts for bulk purchases for sales promotion, premiums, fund-raising, educational, or institutional use.

Special book excerpts or customized printings can also be created to fit specific needs. For details, write or phone the office of the Kensington Special Sales Manager: Kensington Publishing Corp., 119 West 40th Street, New York, NY 10018. Attn. Special Sales Department. Phone: 1-800-221-2647.

eKensington and the K logo Reg. U.S. Pat. & TM Off.

First Electronic Edition: October 2014
eISBN-13: 978-1-60183-359-4
eISBN-10: 1-60183-359-8

First Print Edition: October 2014
ISBN-13: 978-1-60183-363-1
ISBN-10: 1-60183-363-6

Printed in the United States of America

ACKNOWLEDGMENTS

Warm thanks to my gentle and perceptive editor Esi Sogah, who took a chance on a new author and then polished her raw gem until it sparkled.

And to my agent, the charming Sarah E. Younger, who came to my rescue when I was juggling multiple offers.

Thanks K. K. for taking my cop questions seriously, Jenny for her assistance with Spanish—of which I know *nada*—and Caroline, for her excellent suggestions.

To Tom and Jude, for my Nevis atelier. The Porch Seekers: Your insanity keeps me sane!

Hugs to my friends in Central Pennsylvania Romance Writers for lighting the way.

And to my husband . . . my muse . . . my tartan terror. Don't go downtown in your kilt without me.

Dear Reader,

Imagine driving north across the iridescent San Francisco Bay. 'Fog City' melts away, leaving you squinting into that famous California sunshine, the curling ribbon of highway rising . . . falling . . . rising again…until you are held in the embrace of scrubby brown ridges combed with vines, rolling out as far as the eye can see.

Traffic slows. But Napa Valley's reduced speed limit is a blessing. You don't want to miss a single, amazing winery—quaint Victorian to stark minimalist—set among the blocks of grapes.

Or as I like to call them, "wine plants."

From the moment my plane touched down in San Francisco, I sensed my wine country vacation was going to be the start of something magical. I wondered what it would be like to grow up in one of those fabulous mansions. To be born into a deep-rooted American wine dynasty, with all its privileges and drawbacks.

Between tastings, I started scribbling notes about a powerful though flawed patriarch and his beautiful yet conflicted daughters. By the flight home, I was already writing the first pages of *A Taste of Chardonnay*—Book 1 of The Napa Wine Heiresses series.

I hope you'll love reading about how each of the headstrong St. Pierre sisters forges her unique path to love and fulfillment!

All Best,

Heather

CHAPTER 1

Friday, June 13

"Are you my Realtor?"

Chardonnay St. Pierre tried to hide her wariness as she approached the man who'd just stepped out of his retro pickup truck. This wasn't the best section of Napa city.

Their vehicles sat skewed at odd angles in the lot of the concrete building with the AVAILABLE banner sagging along one side. Around the back, gorse and thistles grew waist-high through the cracks in the pavement.

A startlingly white grin spread below the man's aviators.

"Realtor? You waiting for one?"

For the past half hour. "He's late." Char went up on her tiptoes, craning her neck to peer down the street for the tenth time, but the avenue was still empty. She tsked under her breath. She should've taken time after her run to change out of her skimpy running shorts, she thought, reaching discreetly around to give the hems a yank down over her butt. And her Mercedes looked more than a little conspicuous in this neighborhood.

Where was he? She pulled her cell out of her bag to call the Realtor back. But something about the imposing stranger was distracting her, demanding another look. "Have we met?" She squinted, lowering her own shades an inch.

He turned sideways without answering and examined the nondescript building, and when he did, his profile gave him dead away.

Oh my god. Char's breath caught, but he didn't notice. His whole focus was on the real estate. She'd just seen that face smiling out from the *People* magazine at the market over on Solano when she'd picked up some last-minute items for tonight's party.

"What have you got planned for the place?" he asked, totally unselfconsciously.

Then she recovered. To the rest of the world, he was Hollywood's latest It Man. But to Char, he was just another actor. Who happened to have a really great dentist.

"I could ask you the same thing."

"I asked first."

Though she wasn't at all fond of actors, her shoulders relaxed a little. Obviously, she wasn't going to get raped out here in broad daylight by the star of *First Responder*. It was still in theaters, for heaven's sake. He couldn't afford the press.

Still. This building was perfect. And it'd been sitting here empty for the past three years. Just her luck that another party would be interested, right when Char was finally in a position to inquire about it.

To Char's relief, a compact car with a real estate logo plastered from headlights to tailpipe pulled up and a guy in his early thirties bounded out with an abundance of nervous energy.

"This business is *insane*," he said by way of introduction. "Dude calls me from a drive-by and wants me to show it to him, like, *now*, right? So I drop everything, even though I'm swamped with this new development all the way over on Industrial Drive. And then he doesn't show up till quarter of—"

He caught himself, pasted on a proper smile, and extended his hand toward It Man.

"Bill Diamond. And you're Mister . . . ?"

"McBride." The actor shook his hand, then turned and sauntered back to the building with his hands on his hips and his eyes scrutinizing its roofline.

"Ryder McBride?" asked Diamond. *"The* Ryder McBride? Oh!" A smile overspread his face. "Cool! Very cool. Nice to meet you, man." He nodded once for emphasis.

Char stepped up, removing her sunglasses and slipping them over the deep V of her racer-back tee.

"Hi." She thrust out her arm. "I'm—"

The Realtor's eyes grew even wider, as his hand reached for hers. "I know who you are . . . *Chardonnay St. Pierre, right?*"

He was still holding on when Char's phone vibrated in her other palm. One glance at the screen and she sighed.

"Excuse me."

But Diamond didn't let go.

"I've got to take this," she repeated, pronouncing each syllable slow and clear. She gave a little tug, and he came to, his fingers relaxing. "It's my little sister."

She ducked her chin and pressed answer.

"Where are you?" Meri's voice sounded tense.

"Downtown."

"You've got to come meet Savvy and me. Papa's in jail."

Bill Diamond was still gaping when Char dropped her phone into her shoulder bag.

"I'm so sorry. Something important's come up and I have to run."

Like a guy who'd come to expect disappointment at every turn, his face fell. "Oh."

Char felt a stab of empathy.

"Did you want to reschedule?" His brows shot up hopefully.

It was a given. But right now concern for her family eclipsed everything else. "I'll have to call you."

As she turned to go, Ryder spoke up.

"I'm staying. Mind showing me around?"

Char stopped in her tracks halfway to her car and glared back at him. She thought he'd barely noticed her. But she'd swear his broad grin was designed purely to tease.

"Excuse me? This is *my* Realtor."

"Ah, actually . . ." Bill cleared his throat, looked at the ground, and then back up at her. "I work for the seller."

"But *I'm* the one who called you to meet me here," she insisted.

He looked from Char to Ryder and back as he juggled his options, then shrugged. "But you're leaving."

Char's thoughts raced. She hated to leave those two here together, to cook up some deal to steal the building out from under her, but she had no choice. "Fine. Bill, I'll be in touch," she called, climbing into her car, then pulling out of the lot a little too fast.

She loved Papa. Truly, she did. But at times like these, she'd give anything for an ordinary, run-of-the-mill dad, in place of the notorious Xavier St. Pierre.

Chapter 2

The St. Pierre sisters tumbled into the Napa County jail, stopping short at the transparent barrier in front of the reception desk. Char vaguely recalled the floor plan from her last visit. From a holding cell in the rear, they could hear Papa bellowing in his unmistakable Franglais.

"I am American citizen! I have gun license! Wait until my daughter gets here. She is lawyer! I will sue your—"

Papa had always had a flair for the dramatic.

Following an interminable wait during which the incessant click of her older sister's pacing echoed off the tile walls, they were let into a processing area and a young officer holding a clipboard came out to meet them.

"Which one of you is"—he raised the clipboard to eye level and squinted—"Sauvignon?" he said with the audible equivalent of an eye roll.

This guy must be new to the force. The St. Pierres weren't accustomed to going many places in the valley without being recognized.

Savvy stepped forward. "I am."

Thank heavens Savvy was an attorney. Well, almost. She'd recently graduated law school but had yet to take the bar.

"And these are my sisters, Chardonnay and Merlot."

The cop stared.

Was it their fault Papa had named his daughters for grape varietals?

He started to smile, furrowed his brow, and then hitched up his pants with his free hand.

With a half chuckle, he said, "Cheese-oh-man. You can't make this stuff up. Wait till I tell the folks back in Ohio."

"What are the charges, officer?" demanded Savvy—as usual, the designated spokesman. The three women were equally anxious to get past this latest ordeal.

"Well now, let's see here." The cop ticked off the items on his list with maddening slowness. "Discharging a firearm within one hundred yards of a residence. Resisting arrest. Threatening an endangered species was dropped. He's lucky. That would've meant federal charges."

He let the clipboard drop to his side and rocked back on his heels, analyzing the women one by one. His holier-than-thou gaze held a touch of salaciousness. Despite her impatience, Char couldn't help but imagine how they appeared from his perspective.

There was Savvy, whose earlobes sparkled with the full carat diamond studs the girls had received for their sixteenth birthdays. As usual, she wore her auburn hair scraped back into a low, loose knot to show them off. She was dressed tastefully in black from head to toe, as if she'd had a premonition when she got up this morning that she'd be downtown at the police station later that afternoon.

Meri's rich mahogany locks had some new lavender streaks that matched both her T-shirt and sky-high suede wedges. The sound of gunfire must have torn her away from her studio in a state of panic. She hadn't changed out of her paint-flecked shirt.

Last, the cop's gaze scraped over Char's racer back and short shorts, coming to rest on her bare legs. Why did she suddenly feel naked? *Dirty?*

"Sarge says this isn't the first time your old man's been caught shooting at poachers in his koi pond."

Savvy ignored that comment in the interest of expediency.

The policeman disappeared, and after another delay, returned, leading their father. Papa was looking disheveled but still chic in his Italian loafers.

"You can go now, Mr. St. Pierre, until your court date. Meantime, no more shooting at bald eagles. They've recently been taken off the endangered list in California, but you'll find some people around here are fond of them."

Amid a fresh tirade of muttered curses, Char took Papa's elbow, Meri guarded his other flank, and Savvy went ahead.

Char scanned the parking lot.

"Clear," she said, and the four stepped out into the bright sunshine, making a beeline for Char's Mercedes.

But they'd only gone a dozen steps when a guy wielding a long-lensed camera appeared from out of nowhere.

"Xavier! Over here!" he yelled.

"*Dégage!* Get out of here!" Papa lashed out.

"Char! Meri!" the stranger cried out. "What'd he do this time?"

The women averted their eyes and picked up the pace.

"Papa and I will ride with Char," called Savvy to Meri, just before they ducked into the car, taking refuge behind tinted windows.

"Damn police scanners," said Savvy as Char pulled out of the lot. "God's gift to the paparazzi."

Fifteen minutes later, Char pulled into the long white gravel drive of Domaine St. Pierre, just in time for everyone to dress for Papa's big party. It was the first fete of the summer, and Char had been waiting for this particular summer for five long years. Now it was here. Tonight was the night she would give her hometown a taste of a brand-new Chardonnay.

Chapter 3

"Do I seriously have to go to this thing?" Ryder had better things to do than spend his Friday night with a bunch of ritzy people he didn't even know and would probably never meet again. He'd just got off the plane from LAX yesterday to find his mom's gutters needed cleaning and the lawn mowing, and he was anxious to get started on it. And then there was the favor he'd been asked to do by the Firefighters' Relief Fund. But going to the right parties was part of promoting his acting career and arranging the invitations was Amy's job. And he had to admit, one she was damn good at.

"Are you kidding me?" Amy asked, incredulous. "Look, Ryder, I busted my butt finagling this invite. An actor—even a lucky one like you—has to network. You might be a rising star, but a ticket to one of the St. Pierre winery parties is envied up and down the whole north coast. You might meet anyone there, producers to politicians. Of course, they always blend a few mere mortals into the mix. But you have to be on your toes. Tomorrow you could read that the stranger you chatted up during cocktails was a Pulitzer Prize winner, a federal judge, or some rapper on the brink of gold. So hell yes, you have to go. No amount of my hard work will have an effect unless you do your part."

With a sigh, Ryder let himself out of the limo while his driver held the door for Amy, his publicist.

Grimacing as he ran a finger along the inside of his stiff collar, he tipped his head back to take in the sprawling Palladian mansion, surrounded by the manicured gardens of Domaine St. Pierre. A tower of water tumbled down onto itself from a fountain surrounded by an island of flowers that formed a traffic circle in the middle of the driveway.

The uniformed driver got back in the car, and impulsively Ryder turned back and rapped on the tinted glass. When the window slid noiselessly down, he propped a forearm on its edge in a careless stance.

"Thanks for the lift. Stay close in case I decide to bail early."

"Bail early? Hell, if I had the chance to step foot inside St. Pierre's palace, they'd have to pry me out. They say it's all of twenty thousand square feet. Besides that, ol' Xavier knows how to grow 'em. And I don't mean grapes."

"Yeah? I don't know. Any girls who live like this must be pretty stuck on themselves." He lowered his voice even more so his publicist wouldn't hear him over the gurgling fountain and smiled wryly. "The most I'm hoping to get out of this extravaganza is a decent meal." He patted his flat abs. "Amy claims they put out quite a spread."

"Snag me some dessert if you get the chance. I'm partial to cheesecake." The driver grinned, the window slid up again, and Ryder smacked the side of the car as it glided away, forming a slow-moving shadow across the gravel in the glow of the Napa Valley sunset.

Amy waited impatiently, wobbling on sky-high heels. Taking her arm as they navigated the path to the mansion, he tried to recall the briefing she'd given him earlier.

A rising star.

Since that evening when Amy had slipped him her business card as he'd knelt praying in little Saint Joan of Arc, Ryder's life had changed completely. A picture of the interior of the little adobe church flashed through his mind. He could still smell the thick, acrid odor of incense.

It was right after the third annual memorial mass for his dad. Had that been only three years ago? Six in all, since the fire that took his dad's life? It felt like another lifetime.

Mom and the twins had already lit their votives, uttered their closing prayers, and gone, but Ryder couldn't drag himself away. Back then, he had too many problems.

He'd recited the rosary, passing the wooden beads rubbed smooth by his dad's fingers through his own. He'd said the Lord's Prayer. And still he bowed his head, eyes screwed shut, hands now clenched around the beads. Silently pouring out his heart, first to his deceased earthly father and then to his heavenly one. Ryder tried not to think about those days. Why torture himself? But sometimes the memory was too strong. . . .

His head swam with the burden of responsibility. For his mother, trying to make her secretary's salary stretch across mortgage payment, groceries, and utility bills. His brothers, with their bottomless twin appetites for cereal and hamburgers and chips and milk by the gallon. And little Bridget. There were probably lots of things she needed. Girly things, like dresses and shoes and other things that he couldn't even fathom.

He had to do something. But what? He already put in thirty hours a week tending bar. Though that usually made him late to his morning classes, it covered the rent on his dive apartment, and he ate for free.

He could quit college, move home, and tend bar full time. Finishing school would improve his income in the long run, but he was only a junior. His family needed help now.

Then, in the hushed stillness came the sound of high heels on stone. The slow, methodical clicking grew louder, reverberating around the stark adobe walls until, head still downcast, he opened one eye and his sight landed on a well-heeled, feminine foot.

A low voice broke the silence.

"I've been waiting for you in the vestibule, but I can't stay any longer. I have a flight to catch.

"Take your time here. But when you're finished . . . tonight, tomorrow, one day soon . . . I want to talk to you."

Only then did his eyes travel up to her face, but too late—the stranger had already turned away, the click of her shoes receding

*until the heavy wooden door whooshed closed and he was left truly
alone with the smell of frankincense and the weight of his worries.
He looked down at her card. "Amy Smart. Gould Entertainment.
Los Angeles, California."*

Amy. But not the savvy Hollywood-agent Amy he'd come to know.
This was off-duty Amy. The wine-country-tourist-who-had-a-thing-
for-old-churches Amy.

Ryder had barely begun flexing his acting chops when a big studio looking for fresh blood had signed him over all the Daniels,
Roberts, and Zacs for the lead in a film about firefighters.

It was surreal seeing his picture in the celebrity magazines with
the crazy captions: "Ryder McBride Among Hollywood's Hottest,"
"Ryder Sizzles in *First Responder*," and so on. Some of the stories
had a grain of truth to them, but most were pure crap, made up by
agents and journalists to promote careers and sell magazines.

He'd never picked up a gossip rag in his life until his mom and
sister had spotted his photo staring back at them in the grocery store
checkout only a couple of months earlier. They'd called him up in fits
of unintelligible squealing. Ever since, he'd begun to feel as though
he couldn't make a move without somebody taking his picture.

Ryder had always had goals and dreams, but being a movie star
had never been one of them. Neither had partying at a renowned
Napa Valley winery. But his sidestepping hadn't worked with Amy.
After all, he was her pet project. Her very *lucrative* pet project.

"Okay, let's do this," sighed Ryder, as he and Amy crunched
along.

"Now, don't forget," she said under her breath. She counted on her
fingers as she rattled off the St. Pierre sisters' names.

"Meri is the youngest. She's the artsy one. Savvy lives up to her
nickname—brainy. And Chardonnay," Amy said with an eye roll and a
dramatic hand flourish, "is your tall, cool blonde. The middle child,
the do-gooder. Always has her hand in one charity or another. Though,
who knows if it's just a put-on. Personally, I've always thought it was
all orchestrated to compensate for her family's scandals. But then,
that's how my mind works."

"Slow down. What scandals?" asked Ryder, finding it hard to

keep up with her pace, even given those stilettos, and her prattle. His knowledge of the who's who of Napa Valley society was a little thin.

"It's irrelevant." Amy brushed the question off with another impatient flick of her hand. They were climbing the wide marble stairs up to the entrance now.

"Back to the daughters. Take your pick. All three are single, fresh out of college, and it'd be great for you to get hooked up with any one of them in the media."

Her eyes grew large, and she placed a hand on his arm. "Better yet, more than one!"

"Oh, that's just what I want my mom and little sister to read about," Ryder responded drily. He spread his hands, pretending to read a tabloid. " 'Ryder McBride dating not one, but two, of the St. Pierre sisters.' "

"Better yet—all three!" Amy winked.

Ryder winced.

"Try to cooperate. My insider will be watching for any chance to shoot you next to the girls. One good photo sold to *People* is worth a year's pay to a waiter."

As they approached the open double doors where a white-gloved butler waited, Amy gave him one last annoying piece of advice.

"Smile," she said through the clenched teeth of her own wide grin.

Sighing, he dutifully followed suit, in preparation to appear in public. In spite of himself, he was beginning to learn the ropes.

If he was ever going to pay his mom's house off and go back to finish his degree, he had no choice.

Chapter 4

Chardonnay floated through the glittering crowd, stopping every few feet to blow air-kisses and utter warm welcomes.

For as long as she could remember, Papa had been entertaining on June Friday nights to launch the growing season—his contemporary homage to a fertility ritual. As down-to-earth as she was, Char couldn't deny that an invitation to the weekly dinner parties where celebrities, intellectuals, and politicians were entertained was highly coveted. Within minutes of every party ending, the social media sites were hopping with who was there, what they wore, and with whom they left.

Traditionally, the parties began the weekend the girls returned from their respective boarding schools. Over the years, Char and her sisters had met hundreds of accomplished and influential people around the family's long mahogany dining table. But for every worthy guest, there was a shallow, opportunistic social climber. And it wasn't always obvious who was who. Papa, it seemed, had a particularly hard time telling one from the other.

The dinners were both a blessing and a curse. Yet attendance at his parties was virtually the only demand Papa made on his daughters. *Ever.* Besides, they were allowed—encouraged—to invite their own guests, too, which made their annual obligation a little more palatable.

Years of practice had left her perfectly at ease in this setting. Sifting through the bulk of the guests, she soon spotted a regal-looking black woman wearing an understated burgundy suit.

"Dr. Simon!" Char clapped her hands together. "I'm so glad you could come."

"The pleasure is all mine. I believe the last time I saw you was right here at one of your father's dinner parties. You were still in school then. My, how you've grown. You look just like—"

Dr. Simon appeared to bite her tongue. In an obvious attempt to buy time, she took the last sip from her wineglass, the large stones in her rings sparkling.

"Like my mother," Char finished for her, to relieve the older woman of her discomfort.

Maman, the legendary Lily d'Amboise.

Char guided the woman to an overstuffed couch and took a seat at a right angle to her guest. A waiter immediately placed two fresh glasses of wine on a side table.

"It was the year of the McDaniel Foundation's last Napa Charity Challenge—five years ago. I was eighteen. That event made a big impression on me. Ever since, I've been waiting for the chance to be a part of it."

"I'm so pleased that you want to contribute to our work."

"I love the idea of charities competing to win money for their cause," said Char. "Something about it appeals to the competitiveness in me. It doesn't hurt that there's a half-marathon involved, either, since I'm a runner from way back."

"We feel we've developed an original concept. Five years between challenges may seem rather lengthy to some, but the board has discovered that bestowing one extravagant grant every five years, rather than smaller annual grants, has proven to be a greater motivation for the competitors. It's also less of an imposition on donors because they're not being canvassed every year. Even the organizations that don't ultimately win the grant raise a good deal of money for their respective causes."

"I think I read that whoever wins the half-marathon gets a bonus. How does that work? Aren't there usually separate categories for men and women runners?"

"We use a formula that accounts for differences in male/female times to come up with a single winner. Rather like the way golf handicaps work. The foundation grants the one winner of the race a fifty-thousand-dollar donation toward his or her charity's total earnings," said Dr. Simon.

"I think I've already memorized every detail of the contest, but can we talk specifically about the gala?" So far, this night was unfolding exactly as Char had hoped. It was all about face time with Dr. Simon. Relationship building.

"Before the half-marathon, the participants are given two weeks to solicit suitable items for the auctions. The race is held on the morning of the final day, followed by the black tie gala, which consists of dinner, dancing, and both silent and live bidding. The whole thing is a tremendous amount of work for those in charge of the competing charities."

"I presume that's another benefit of having it only once every five years," said Char.

Dr. Simon nodded. "That's right. Tell me, is there any particular cause you're interested in working with for your very first challenge? The food bank? Perhaps the women's shelter? Any of our partner organizations would be thrilled to have you. I'd be more than happy to make some calls, set up an introduction."

Char scooted forward. Time for her speech. She hoped she didn't look as nervous as she felt.

"I've been wanting to talk to you about that. Ever since I was a teenager, I've been involved with a bunch of causes during the summer months, getting my feet wet. I've served at the soup kitchen, done some fund-raising, and I still help sort donations at church."

Dr. Simon nodded politely.

"In every place that I volunteered, I watched and listened. And I noticed that a large percentage of underprivileged people were the children of pickers—er, excuse me, that's what Papa calls them. You know what I mean. Migrant farmworkers. Immigrants."

"Go on," said Dr. Simon.

"I got to know some families when I was serving at the soup kitchen. Then I started working at Saint Joan of Arc. There, I learned that more people would've come to the mission, but they didn't have transportation. That's when I started driving donations over to their neighborhoods. I found out firsthand: It's all about outreach.

"When I went back to college in the fall, I couldn't forget those kids. There were two especially whose faces kept me up at night, wondering and worrying. I couldn't wait to graduate and make public service my career. So I did some research and found that Napa already had well-established organizations for the hungry, the homeless, the addicted, and various medical conditions. But I wanted to do something specifically for migrant children. These are the children of the vineyards. And wine is the basis of the valley's economy."

She took a sip of her wine, hoping she wasn't running on. She had to say this right. Competing in the challenge meant everything to her.

"As you know, I'm one of the lucky ones. A third-generation landowner. My family's business has always been intertwined with migrant workers. I feel compelled to do something for their kids."

Dr. Simon's expression was interested but guarded.

"So I've started my own foundation."

There—she'd said it. Despite Dr. Simon's cool poise, her eyebrows rose sharply. Char rushed on before she could be shot down.

"I even found a building that would be perfect to work out of, right in the center of an immigrant neighborhood. And I've recruited a group to run in the half-marathon with me: the local women's field hockey team I play on every summer. I think it'll be easier to persuade people to contribute to my cause if I'm an actual participant, instead of just an organizer, don't you? We started training separately months ago, while I was still in school. Now we can finally start running together, as a real team. . . ."

A hint of a shadow swept across the professor's face then, as if she'd suddenly remembered exactly whose couch she sat on, and Char's heart sank. She'd seen that look on plenty of faces before.

All of her life, people had made assumptions about Char, simply because she was one of the three granddaughters of Yves St. Pierre, the Burgundian winemaker who'd brought French cultivars to California and planted them here one hundred years ago.

It was Papa's favorite story, one his daughters and all his workers, from head winemaker to lowly picker, knew by heart. Yves had survived the dry times by selling inferior communion wine for a premium and stockpiling the good stuff. He knew Prohibition would eventually be repealed, and the minute it was, he had a cellar full of mature cabernet ready to meet demand. Now, a century later, the award-winning Domaine St. Pierre label was celebrated from Napa to Paris.

But there was a downside to being a St. Pierre. Char's individuality went largely unrecognized. Her mind, her values, and her feelings were all obscured by the family's success—and their equally tragic mistakes—over the decades.

As she'd matured, even Char's physical appearance had become a handicap, to her way of thinking. Some might think being a skinny blue-eyed blonde was an asset, but Char worried that it only added to people's impression of her as an empty-headed heiress. She would have competed in sports even if she *hadn't* had long muscles and a high metabolism, but sports fed her need for legitimacy apart from her looks. She'd played field hockey all her life and was honored when the local women agreed to run with her for the challenge.

"Dr. Simon, I can't blame you for what you're thinking—that Papa could easily underwrite my entire campaign. But I've made a decision. I want to raise all of my contributions myself, solely from the fundraising events. Independent of the St. Pierre name."

Dr. Simon looked doubtful.

Char couldn't use her trust fund, either. That wasn't technically hers until she was thirty. She felt her chin harden, and a vision of Papa's own set jaw flashed through her memory. She winced. Stubbornness was the least pretty trait she'd inherited, but you couldn't choose your genes.

"There's no need to rush to that decision—" Dr. Simon advised, but Char interrupted.

"I've made up my mind. I'm only going to use the proceeds from the official events, like all the other contenders. Every penny I get for my cause will be earned."

"You realize that you'll be up against some stiff competition. The challenge always attracts the most established charities in the county. Have you even filed paperwork to—"

"But that's what makes it so exciting!" Char cut in. "The chance to prove my new organization on the same playing field with those other institutions is even more incentive for me to enter."

"Are you quite sure? There are already a dozen well-established causes in the valley that I'm sure would be thrilled to have you on their team. Does this budding organization of yours have a name yet?"

"I was thinking about 'Valley Kids.' "

Dr. Simon's brows knit. "Somewhat generic, don't you think? If you insist on forming your own foundation, why not use your name recognition to advantage? Say, 'Chardonnay's Children'?"

Char bristled. "Doesn't that sound a little egotistical? I'm not doing this to draw attention to myself." That was the *last* thing she wanted. "It's for those kids."

"Not at all. In my opinion, it's always wise to utilize whatever advantages one has at her disposal. Your name is distinctive. It carries a whiff of the St. Pierre prestige, which you must admit, is considerable here in the valley. Yet it doesn't allude to your last name outright. The word *chardonnay* even has a double meaning. It's more than your name; it's also a widely grown varietal. The benefits will be worth the off chance that you'll be thought conceited for using your name in the title."

" 'Chardonnay's Children.' " Char tried it out on her tongue.

"And one never knows. Rather than making you sound egotistical, it may have a positive effect on your family's reputation."

That was a tactfully veiled reference to the less savory part of her family's past. Maman's vanishing act and what came after. Papa's philandering and arrest record. Embarrassing scandals she'd had nothing to do with that made her cringe just thinking of them.

Dr. Simon's warm expression returned, and she leaned over and touched Char's hand maternally.

"In the end, it's your foundation, your choice. Give it some thought. In any case, I admire your modesty and your enthusiasm, my dear. Even if you decide to join an established cause and wait until the next challenge to start your own concern. No one would think any less of you."

Char looked up to see a distinguished looking man with silver hair.

"Nicole!" The man bent down and kissed Dr. Simon's cheek.

"Winston! How lovely to see you!"

Char excused herself for the time being. She'd left explicit instructions to the staff to seat the head of the McDaniel Foundation directly across from her at dinner. She had all night to cement a bond with the woman she wanted desperately for her career coach and mentor.

Chapter 5

Ryder took a tentative sniff of the straw-colored wine he'd been offered by a circulating butler. His substantial hand contrasted with the thin, brittle crystal, and for a second he wondered if he held the glass in the proper way.

Amy drew Ryder's attention to two women—one fair, the other dark—from where they sat across the well-appointed room.

"That's Chardonnay," hissed Amy. "Next to her is Nicole Simon, chair of the McDaniel Foundation."

Angled in a chair next to a middle-aged African-American lady sat the woman he'd bumped into that very afternoon on Pueblo Avenue. She'd changed into a drapey white dress that obscured her slim physique. Huge, silver circles pierced her ears and a silver cross hung between her breasts.

What did Chardonnay St. Pierre want with a run-down warehouse on the poor side of town?

But almost equally as intriguing to Ryder was the presence of Dr. Simon. Maybe this dinner party wouldn't be such a bore after all.

Amy snatched something that resembled a fried bird's nest from the tray of a passing waiter. "Did you manage to switch the names on the place settings?" she whispered.

"Swapped Ryder McBride and Nicole Simon," replied the waiter, without moving his lips.

"Excellent," muttered Amy.

"Mingle, mingle!" she then sang out to Ryder. "I'm going to work this crowd like a sheepdog on steroids. Watch and learn."

All the introductions had been made and a dozen bottles of the latest vintage poured. Orange rays of late-day sunlight streaming through the tall windows flattered the guests' complexions as they made their way into the softer glow of the candlelit dining room. Inhibitions were falling away, and voices rose above the clatter of silver on china and the clink of fine crystal.

"Ry!"

As soon as Ryder saw the redhead seated to his right, he groaned inwardly. She'd had a small part in his last movie and had been chasing him ever since.

"Miranda." Ryder nodded and immediately averted his eyes, hoping she wouldn't start with her usual antics. But before the first course had even been served, she had her hand on his thigh under the table. He promptly reached down and removed it, but to no avail. She put it back, higher this time. He shoved it away more firmly. There was nothing more he could do without causing a scene, and even though the house he'd grown up in was about a tenth the size of this one, his mother had raised him better than that.

The actor with the radiant teeth reached his long arm across the table to briefly grasp Char's hand.

"We were never properly introduced. Ryder McBride. Thanks for the invite. Nice place you got here."

Despite the warmth of his hand, Char's smile felt tight. Inside, she was seething. It wasn't that Ryder McBride had been invited to the party. That was no surprise; Papa loved all things Hollywood.

What bugged her was that Nicole Simon was supposed to be sitting across from her, not him. Somehow, Dr. Simon had ended up way down at the other end, where Char couldn't possibly get to know her better. And getting to know Nicole Simon tonight was priority one. She considered correcting the error, but she wouldn't dream of risking embarrassing her guests.

Second, there was no one Char wanted to sit across from less than Tinseltown's latest hottie. Other than the fact that they were both interested in buying the same building, she didn't know much about him. But judging from most of the other beautiful male actors she'd met at Papa's parties, he was guaranteed to be a self-centered egomaniac.

Besides, she'd had enough of actors to last a lifetime. It wasn't enough that her own mother had been one—before abandoning the family. It seemed as though every time she turned around, Papa had a new actress clinging to his arm or lying about their pool, downing wine by the barrel. Papa had always had an infatuation with film people. And they, in turn, had always been drawn to the wine country.

The girls were encouraged to invite their own guests to these affairs, but they had no veto power over their father's choices.

Looking around their end of the long table for anyone who would listen, the overly sequined young woman next to Ryder pronounced, "Ryder and I go way back. We worked together in *First Responder*. Didn't we, Ry?" She giggled, wrapping her hands around his bicep and drawing Char's attention to its toned thickness.

Sequin Girl drained her glass and reached over for Ryder's. "You won't mind if I have a teensy sip of yours, will you?" She leaned into him, lifting her doe eyes.

Ignoring her, Char glared evenly at Ryder with barely disguised disdain.

"There's a merlot coming with the tuna," she said, nodding toward the empty balloon-shaped goblet sitting above his plate. "Papa likes to offer a different house wine with every course."

"It's okay. She can have mine," Ryder said, brazenly matching Char's glare while sliding his own full glass of white to his right until it was in front of the starlet's place setting.

Miranda perked up suddenly. "Hey! I heard your dad got arrested today. Did you hear that, Ry? For shooting a bald eagle." Miranda pointed a pretend rifle skyward. "*Bang!* Did he kill the poor thing?"

The other guests averted their eyes, and Char's cheeks warmed. But before she could come up with a retort, Miranda's mind had already flitted onto something else, as evidenced by her whispering into Ryder's ear. Signs of a scuffle erupted under the tablecloth, the Belgian white linen being pulled between Ryder and his costar.

Char fought to hide a scowl. Couldn't these Hollywood types keep their hands off each other for five minutes? But then she cringed inwardly. Maman had been one of those Hollywood types.

To Char's relief, Ryder redirected the conversation with what seemed to be an honest attempt at civility. "Isn't that Nicole Simon sitting at the far end of the table?"

Char's defenses rose another notch. "You know Nicole Simon?"

"I know *of* her. But I've always wanted to meet her."

"You must have Dr. Simon confused with someone else. *This* Dr. Simon is a professor of humanities at San Jose State, as well as the chairwoman of the McDaniel Foundation," Char said with some satisfaction.

A ruddy-cheeked woman with a thick middle blustered up behind Ryder's chair. In her trembling hand were a pen and scrap of paper.

"I'm so sorry to bother you, Mr. McBride, but may I have your autograph? It's for my niece. She loved you in *First Responder*."

Ryder seemed genuinely surprised by the request.

"I was in *First Responder*, too," piped in Sequin Girl.

The woman gave her a quick once-over and turned back to her original target.

"What's your niece's name?" Ryder asked. He scribbled something in response and handed it back with a dazzling smile. The tickled guest scurried back to her seat.

Char sighed. As little respect as she had for actors, she still empathized with them when they couldn't find a moment's peace, even in a private home. Incidents like the one she'd just witnessed didn't happen often at the mansion. Most of their guests were far too sophisticated to fawn over famous people, even if they were secretly dazzled.

"Sorry," said Ryder to those around him. "That's only the third time in my life I've ever been asked for an autograph. I'd have felt guilty turning her down."

His perfect mouth curved into a sheepish grin. In spite of her preconceived opinions, Char's heart began to thaw a little.

The balding county commissioner to her left leaned over and said, "He'd better get used to it. My fifteen-year-old daughter can't stop talking about him."

"Well, maybe Mr. McBride will be kind enough to give you his autograph, too—to take home to your daughter, of course," Char said, looking pointedly at Ryder. She was still perturbed that she had to spend the whole evening across from an actor, contrary to plan.

"I wasn't asking—wouldn't want to interrupt his dinner again," sputtered the commissioner.

Ryder nodded. "Not a problem, Commissioner Jones. I voted for you. I liked your stance on the highway bill. Be glad to sign something for your daughter."

The man, clearly as starstruck as any teenage girl, drew his card from his shirt pocket and handed it to Ryder.

Char picked at her salad. It would be up to her to introduce a topic more substantial than autographs into the conversation. She turned to the commissioner.

"Speaking of fifteen-year-olds, would you happen to have any statistics on the number of migrants under the age of eighteen in the county? I'm doing some research for a charity I'm involved with."

"I could give you some rough numbers, but I'd have to check the latest figures. May I have my assistant get back to you next week?"

"Are you talking strictly Latinos?" asked Ryder.

Char's and Jones's heads swiveled simultaneously toward him.

"According to the latest census, half the kids in Napa County schools are from Mexican families. That number's tripled over the last decade. Ninety percent of those kids were born here. But the number could be even bigger, since there're kids who are invisible—not enrolled in school."

"Er—that sounds about right," stuttered Jones.

"Of those who are orphans, sixty-five percent of their parents died from disease-related deaths. Fifteen percent from traffic accidents, ten in farm-related accidents, and ten in fires."

Char blinked, nonplussed.

"Of those who died in fires, about half had no smoke alarms."

The commissioner cleared his throat and fiddled uneasily with his silverware.

"I daresay that figure is probably standard across the state, despite persistent public service announcements every spring and fall instructing people to buy new batteries for their smoke alarms."

"But how many of those migrant households speak Spanish? They might not understand the PSAs if they're in English," said Char.

"Exactly. I've read that the percentage of students living in what is called 'linguistically isolated' families is three times higher in California than the rest of the country," said Ryder. "What I find most surprising is that thirty percent of the kids with limited English are third-generation immigrants. They've gone to school here all their lives, but they're still deficient because they speak a different language at home."

Miranda, looking bored, switched her boozy focus to the shy St. Pierre accountant sitting on her opposite side. Char smiled inwardly as she watched him grow rattled by the starlet's attention.

Char, Ryder, and the commissioner talked demographics right through the cheese course. It was so engrossing, it almost compensated for not sitting by Dr. Simon.

"I'll call you next week with those figures," said Commissioner Jones as dessert was served.

"That'd be great. I'm especially interested in migrant housing demographics. From what I've read, inexpensive housing options are scarce, especially Upvalley."

Despite her preconceptions, Char couldn't help but be impressed by Ryder McBride. There was no possible way he could've known he'd be seated across from a Napa County commissioner at dinner or prepared for the topics that had come up.

Or could he? Someone had switched his seat with Nicole Simon, after all. Char's suspicions came flooding back.

Yet even if it had been Ryder who'd done the switching, she was still curious about his depth of knowledge.

She studied him as he dug into his cheesecake, wishing too late that she'd had the caterer do a second dessert. She was dying for some chocolate.

Then she straightened. He might be well informed. But he was still an actor. For that reason alone, Ryder McBride couldn't be trusted.

Chapter 6

Contrary to all his expectations, Ryder had thoroughly enjoyed himself so far. Between the great food, meeting his favorite local politician, and getting to feast his eyes on Chardonnay St. Pierre all night, he'd completely forgotten that he'd been dreading this event.

Even the irritating Miranda had disappeared into the crowd, presumably to look for a more willing victim—er, partner.

"Char," as she was called, was pretty down-to-earth, for a winery heiress. He'd been surprised by her brains, even if she had looked down her nose at him at first. But he couldn't fault her for that. Who wouldn't have been put off with the autograph hounds and his drunken neighbor crawling all over him?

That's when it hit him. He had just entered a phase in his life in which everybody he met would fall into one of two camps: those who were—crazily enough—in awe of him, and those who'd underestimate him. All because he'd made it big, right out of the gate.

His PR agent had been seated far down the table, but now she approached him with questioning eyes, shaking Ryder from his thoughts. He hadn't maneuvered any of the St. Pierre girls into a photo op, and it was getting late. Some people were already drifting toward the door. She wasn't going to be happy.

"Well?" Amy mouthed.

Ryder scanned the room. A loosely organized line of people had formed to kiss the scented air around Char and her sisters, and shake the hand of their proud "Papa."

"Need a little more time. Where's our server?"

"Over there, waiting to clear the tables." Amy pointed with her chin toward a corner of the room.

"Ask him to wrap me up a hunk of cheesecake to go. Then tell him to be ready to shoot as I say good night."

Amy tossed him a look that said if he let her down there'd be hell to pay.

He hung in the shadows of the flickering candlelight, studying Char's every nuance as her guests lined up to say their good-byes. She was a fine-boned, vulnerable-looking thing—as delicate as his wineglass, despite her height and her cool, confident demeanor. Her eyebrows were darker than her blond hair. He squinted. The sprinkling of freckles across her straight nose that he'd first noticed during dinner weren't visible from this distance. But those lips couldn't be missed. They were the color of ripe watermelon. Full in the center, her top lip swooped down, then up again at the edges, in a perpetual, slight smile. And the pillowy bottom one? That was killing him. He wondered what it would feel like to suck on. Soft and lush and . . .

And what? What the hell was he thinking?

Tossing back the last of his drink, he noticed again his own hand cradling the glass. Like that expensive crystal, Char would require gentle handling. Out of nowhere, a primitive surge of protectiveness washed over him.

He stepped into place at the end of the dwindling line.

Something was happening inside of Ryder. Out of the blue, every atom in his being went on high alert. This formal farewell was designed to appease Amy. He was only doing his duty by getting near enough to his hostess to be photographed for the press coverage. So why was his pulse racing like he'd just run a mile uphill? Why couldn't he breathe right?

Then it hit him like a brick between the eyes, and he knew. The past two hours sitting across from Char had changed everything. She was crazy gorgeous. And brainy. And to top it all off, she shared his passion for helping people, a trait that was completely lacking in the women who'd been falling all over him since he'd moved to LA.

He felt pressured to pack all the right things into this one moment. His job was pleasing Amy with a photo people would be talking about tomorrow. But more importantly, he had to impress Char. Because he had to see her again. *Had to.* But with all his blood flowing out of his brain and into his crotch, he suddenly couldn't think.

"It was very nice meeting you, Char."

"You too, *Ry,*" she teased, playfulness sparkling in her blue eyes. "I enjoyed talking with you."

With a tilt of her head, she turned suddenly serious. "Before you go, what was the building like? Did you go inside? What's the asking price?"

That top lip curved way up into an innocent-looking smile, but her eyes betrayed her. She was a shrewd competitor.

"Whoa! That's a lot of questions. You never answered mine earlier. What's your interest in it?"

This time she didn't hesitate. "A place to house my charitable foundation for migrant children. You?"

"My Realtor advised me to keep my plans under my hat," he replied. He heard himself speaking but had no idea where his words were coming from.

"*Your* Realtor?" she gasped.

"You left. I stayed. You know what they say: location, location, location."

Her eyebrows came together. "But that's not what that expression means . . ."

Stupid! He shrugged it off, then forged ahead. This was it. He took her hand. But instead of merely shaking it, he folded her into him, bored his eyes into hers, wrapped his other arm around her waist, and zoned in on that impossibly lush mouth of hers.

Click.

Chapter 7

The article under the splashy, front-page photograph read:

Ryder McBride: Drunk on Chardonnay?

The break-out star of First Responder apparently has a taste for the good stuff . . . the very good stuff.

Last night he was photographed swapping saliva with winery heiress Chardonnay St. Pierre at one of her father's fabulous Friday night fetes.

This, despite the fact that McBride's dinner companion was flame-haired costar Miranda Hempt.

Only last week, Ryder was spotted with "Tipsy" Rodriguez at a Los Angeles party.

The break-out star is playing the field in more ways than one. On top of his scalding hot social life, Ryder is set to begin filming Triple Play this month. The story is based on the Los Angeles Angels, but will be shot in Ryder's hometown of Napa city. His role requires the already buff six-foot-four actor to change up his workouts in order to channel a professional baseball pitcher.

Char, as the middle St. Pierre daughter is known, is the blond celebutante who's been seen hopscotching between an assortment of causes, from animal shelters to food banks, during her summers off from the University of Connecticut.

Ms. St. Pierre—and her sisters, who are also named after noble grapes—normally shun the limelight. On those rare occasions when they're spotted out, their beauty and style inspire envy in women and admiration in men.

As children, their father sent them away following the untimely death of their mother, Academy Award–winning actress Lily d'Amboise, purportedly on the advice of well-meaning friends. But wine country residents have been quietly watching them for years, like all fine wines, just waiting for them to mature.

Their buzz has been slowly fermenting until this spring, when an invitation to rub shoulders with the St. Pierres at one of their father's spring galas has become the social coup of the season.

Watch out, Napa! It's gonna be a long, hot summer!

" *'CELEBUTANTE?'* " exclaimed Char when Savvy showed her the photograph on her tablet the next day during breakfast.

It hadn't been the way it looked in print. She stared some more at the screen. It had really only been a two-second meeting of lips. Hadn't it? Yet in the photo, the way he had her bent backward, with his head to the side, his arm snaked around her waist, the long lashes of his closed eyelids splayed across his high cheekbones, it looked as though Ryder McBride had swept her off her feet.

"Ooooooh! Can you believe the nerve of that man?" Char cried.

"Hey, it was the reporter who called you a celebutante, not Ryder. Actually, you guys look really good together—that is, speaking strictly from an aesthetic standpoint," said Meri coolly, examining the photo with her artist's eye, tilting her head this way then that.

"Do you want me to file suit?" teased Savvy, snatching a gold pen from a drawer that glided quietly on its track.

Char sniffed.

"No lawsuits! That's the last thing this family needs: more negative publicity."

With a Mona Lisa smile, Savvy sat back in her seat, arms folded. "And no, we do not look good together," she informed Meri.

Although that wasn't altogether true. Actually, they did look nice together. In fact, their bodies seemed to fit together perfectly. The longer she studied the photo, the more her stomach fluttered. But she'd never admit it aloud.

Char tossed the iPad back at Meri, who caught it just in time and continued with her critique.

"It's a little photoshopped," said Meri. "Obviously, whoever took it couldn't use a flash or he would've been noticed, so he doctored the exposure."

"I just can't believe he did that," Char muttered as she paced across the cavernous kitchen designed to resemble an updated chateau. "Went to such great lengths to pass himself off as sincere, when he's clearly just another scammer manipulating me for a photo op."

"Now, how do you know that? Maybe he's both," said Meri.

"A sincere scammer? That's an oxymoron," said Savvy.

"He's a moron, all right. I wonder if any one of those facts and figures he threw out at dinner were true, or just made up."

She'd know soon enough, when Commissioner Jones got back to her.

"I don't see you fighting it," shot back Meri, still studying the picture.

Ouch.

Then Savvy chimed in. "Actually, I don't think many people at the party even noticed much. Most of them had already left at that point, and Papa's back was turned. And those who did see it must have assumed it was no big deal because I didn't hear anyone remark on it."

Neither had Char. But then, Char had been in a complete daze, barely able to stumble upstairs to her suite, when the good-night kiss—or whatever it was intended to be—was through.

Before yesterday, if anyone had told Chardonnay St. Pierre that she would have permitted a virtual stranger to kiss her like that in public—or in private, for that matter—without slapping him all the way to Sacramento . . . well, it was inconceivable.

But for some unfathomable reason, she *had* allowed it. Had melted right into his arms.

It hadn't been just the kiss itself. It'd been the passionate, yet controlled way Ryder had delivered it that had blown her away.

From the very outset, she'd found him way more intriguing than she'd cared to admit. He'd surprised her with his depth and intellect at the table. Sexy, charismatic guys like Ryder McBride weren't supposed to have brains or care about social causes.

Later, as he'd taken those long, slow strides toward her before saying good night, he'd paralyzed her with a hypnotic stare from deep, liquid eyes. She'd been jelly by the time she heard the skin-on-skin clap of his warm, firm hand on hers, coupling it in a warm, perfect fit.

The decisiveness in his muscular arm as he'd drawn her into him, as if she already belonged to him . . . had *always* belonged to him . . . won over her body to the complete exclusion of her mind.

Her mind. Something in the back of it, like a separate witness to what was happening, had been aghast at the sheer nerve of him! Yet, it was as if they'd floated onto another plane together, apart from the rest of the universe.

Even now, she still wasn't sure how long she'd been in his arms; time had been suspended when her body was pressed against his.

"Let me see that again." Char reached for the reader with an inexplicable urge to study the picture's every nuance. It was a visual record of last night. She was mortified to realize that the photo would live forever online, perversely enabling her to obsess over it as often as she wanted.

All she'd had to go on before was how the kiss had *felt.* Now that she had the picture, she studied it from an onlooker's perspective.

From the moment Ryder had asserted himself, she'd succumbed to his charm. His mouth had taken complete possession of hers; there was no other way to describe it. His lips had brushed hers, warm, soft, and barely parted, but after the initial contact, had prodded, coaxing hers open. When she did, he'd nudged in farther with his chin, eager for her as a hungry but gentle bear. Nudging her wider with a shallow sweep of his tongue, which tasted like the strawberry cheesecake they'd just consumed. Opening, closing, seducing. She'd given herself up to the strength of his arms holding her captive . . . limply followed his every lead.

Like some lame-brained actress in a bad movie, she now realized. How could she be so gullible?

And then, when she would've done anything to make him go on, he'd pulled back, leaving her utterly breathless.

But before he let her go, they'd locked eyes again, until she became aware of his breath on her damp lips and glanced down at the wet gleam on his own mouth. He'd flicked just the tip of his tongue across his lower lip then, as if to taste the residue of her. From within the warmth of his chest, his heart—or was it hers?—pounded.

Char had been analyzing it all night, the memory twirling about in her head as her body twisted the sheets.

By dawn, she'd figured out the real reason she'd let him get away with it.

It was the suspicion that Ryder had been as shocked by his own action as she'd been by her *re*action. That it hadn't been planned; he hadn't merely been taking advantage of circumstances.

Hours of tossing and turning deluded her into believing that maybe—just *maybe*—the good-looking, intelligent-despite-being-an-actor Ryder McBride might truly have kissed her not because she was a social climber's wet dream, but out of genuine desire.

But now, in the light of morning—and the reader—she saw his behavior for what it obviously was: a setup. A publicity ploy, designed to get him juicy press.

"I'm going for a run," Char announced, slamming the kitchen door behind her.

But not before she called Bill Diamond again. That building was perfectly situated for her plans. And no mere actor was going to snatch it away from her, no matter how good a kisser he was.

Chapter 8

"*Mom!* Look at this! Hurry up and look!" Bridget sat at the family computer in her flannel pj's. A cartoon was playing softly on the TV over by the couch when Ryder entered his family living room, yawning.

"Bridget, how many times have I asked you not to eat cereal at the computer? If you spill milk into the keyboard, it'll be ruined," his mother scolded, drying her hands on a tea towel.

The girl hurriedly set her bowl on the coffee table, milk swirling perilously close to its rim, and tugged urgently on the sleeve of her mother's robe. "Come 'ere! You gotta see this picture of Ryder!"

"What picture?" he interjected, scratching his torso.

Neither female responded. Both of their heads were bowed over the screen.

"'Ryder McBride: Drunk on Chardonnay?'" quoted Bridget, mispronouncing Char's name with a hard *ch*. She lifted her face to his, and her youthful innocence tore at something inside him.

Bridget was the baby of the family. Ben and Brian, his twin brothers, had just gotten home for the summer, but today was Saturday. They wouldn't be up for another hour.

"What does that mean? Were you really drunk? Is that why you're kissing that girl?"

Then his mother gave him the same vexed expression she'd worn when he'd broken his arm riding his dirt bike off a homemade ramp at age thirteen.

Nothing like that look to wake up a guy fast.

Only nine hours earlier, he'd been at that high-class party, rubbing shoulders with politicians and socialites.

"Let me see that." Ryder nosed in between them. He skimmed the story. But what caught his attention was the photo.

He had to admit, it was good. It resurrected something pleasurable in his gut. And below the drawstring in his pajama bottoms. He shifted his hips a little, hoping no one would notice.

"Well, Amy should be pleased," he muttered.

That had been the prime objective of last night: to be seen in public with one of the St. Pierre heiresses.

Though kissing Chardonnay had ignited something exciting deep within him, he wasn't fool enough to think it'd go any further. Especially once she saw this. Any slim chance he might've hoped for to see her again was gone like that slab of cheesecake he'd snuck out to the limo driver, via Amy's colossal handbag.

"Who's Amy?" asked Bridget, pointing to the screen. "Her?"

"No, not her. Amy's my PR person. That's Chardonnay."

"But why should she be happy? Amy, I mean?" pressed Bridget.

The toast popped up, and his mother left the computer and returned to the kitchen to butter it.

Ryder sighed, opened the fridge to get some orange juice, and tried to think of a way to explain to an inquisitive eleven-year-old why getting his picture taken kissing a rich society girl he barely knew would help pay their mortgage and utility bill.

"First things first," he said, downing his juice in one gulp. "I wasn't drunk, not in the least. Second, that girl's name is Chardonnay," he said, enunciating clearly. "She's just a friend of mine."

"Like the other ones I read about online and in those magazines at the grocery store?" replied Bridget.

"Yep. Just like those. Same thing."

Bridget looked doubtful.

He tried again. "See, when people read stories about me, it makes them want to watch my movies. And the more people who go to my movies, the more money I get. That's how actors get paid. And if I get my picture taken with pretty girls, that makes me seem much more interesting."

"The kids at school say you have lots of girlfriends."

"Nope. None of those girls in the pictures are my girlfriends."

"That's what I told them, but they don't believe me."

"That's okay. I only care about what you and Mom think. And I always tell you two the truth." He could have included the bros in that pronouncement, but at nineteen, they had a healthy preoccupation with sports, cars, and *real* girls. Celebrity gossip was way off their radar.

"But you were kissing her." Bridget frowned.

She was right. Though there'd been other published photos with him around women, this was the first shot of him in an actual embrace—as far as he knew. He only read about himself when other people brought it to his attention.

"That's enough, Bridget," his mother said from over at the stove. "Do you two want some eggs?"

Bridget shook her head and went back to her preoccupation with the computer while Ryder ran his hand through his sleep-tousled hair and groaned. He was in warrior mode for this film, but he couldn't say no to his mom's cooking.

"Okay. Then I'm going for a run. I'll be back later to mow the grass. I canceled the lawn service for the summer, since I'll be staying here till the film's in the can."

Chapter 9

Ryder parked along a flat stretch of a two-lane road near his favorite running trail. He was on mile two when Amy called.

"Did you see?" she squealed.

"I saw. Surprised you waited so long to call."

"I know, right? Oh my god, what a great picture. I couldn't have staged that better if I'd posed you myself. I gave them more information, but they didn't use it. Maybe next time. I found out where they hang. You know, the St. Pierres. Bouchon Bakery for their TLC cookies, Bottega for dinner—"

"Amy . . ." He kept his voice steady. She was the third woman he'd had to contend with today and it wasn't even noon. "There's not going to be a next time. It's a safe bet Chardonnay St. Pierre hates my guts."

"What? Giving up so soon? Listen, I heard they're going to be at Diablo next Fri—"

But now Ryder was distracted by a group of women approaching at a right angle.

"Hey," he puffed. "I'm running. Remember? Got to get in shape for this new film. Call you later."

"Running? Oh, that's why you're breathing so hard. Yes, that's important. You go work those glutes."

He slipped his phone into his pocket, then slowed as he approached the intersection.

The group reached the corner just in front of him and turned onto his path.

"Three-mile mark!" A strikingly familiar voice came from a lithe runner with a blond ponytail. Its owner looked his way without breaking stride—until her face froze with recognition.

"I take it you saw the photo," Ryder said, matching her gait as he ran up alongside her.

After her morning, Char had just begun to calm down. Now her anger reared up all over again. Too furious to respond, she focused on maintaining her pace and stared straight ahead, though she was aware of heat creeping up on her face. Her fair coloring was conducive to blushing, and the realization that Ryder McBride might notice her anger made her even madder.

Up ahead, none of her teammates noticed anything unusual. But then, none of them had been present at last night's dinner at the mansion, nor apparently seen the evidence on the Internet—or were too considerate to mention it. But Char knew it was only a matter of time.

"Just so you know, hellcat, it wasn't my idea," said Ryder.

"I'm not your hellcat. And what wasn't your idea? The kiss? Or the picture?" Char fought to appear unruffled, but both of them were already breathing hard from running.

"None of it."

She gave him a scathing sideways glance. "Well then, whose idea was it?"

Ryder dodged a big crack in the sidewalk, then wove back.

Then they both started talking at once.

He began apologizing, as she added, "What even made you want to come last night in the first place?"

"I didn't."

Char turned and viewed him with undisguised amazement. And when she did, she couldn't help but notice the muscles in his arms and across his chest, under the thin fabric of his shirt. He wasn't musclebound, but he was very fit and his proportions were perfect.

"Going to your party was never my idea. My PR person managed to get an invite through your father's people."

Char could hardly keep from rolling her eyes. He was so typical, predictable Hollywood.

"But once you got your foot in the door, you thought, why not capitalize on your visit by making a play for the hostess—for the camera?"

"Look, I'm not going to make excuses. Yes, I went to your party on the advice of my agent. But the kiss? That was all my idea. Not even Martin Scorsese could have made me kiss you if I hadn't wanted to."

"Well, I hope you enjoyed it."

"As a matter of fact, I did enjoy it. I enjoyed it immensely." His smile lit up his whole face.

Char noticed she'd broken a sweat from exertion—or was it because of the guy running next to her, matching her step for step? Char was a seasoned runner, but surely Ryder had slowed his usual pace to stay next to her, a woman. With those quads, he could've left her in the dust by now. What was his motivation? He had to know she'd never allow a repeat of last night. Never in a million, billion years.

"Well, that was the first and last time you'll ever kiss me."

"Yeah, that's what I figured. 'Specially after I saw the picture. Only 'cause my baby sister showed it to me. Personally, I have better things to do than look myself up online."

Char was about to deliver a severe tongue-lashing when her media radar went on alert.

"What are you doing here, anyway?" she asked suspiciously.

He shrugged, smiled, and faked an innocent look. "Uh . . . running?"

"What are you *really* doing? How'd you find me?"

"I didn't 'find' you. I wasn't even looking for you."

"Right. How naive do you think I am? Where are they?"

She twisted sideways, then made a full circle while jogging in place, searching for bushes or slow-moving cars.

"Where are who? The paparazzi?" He snorted. "Look, hellcat, you might be beautiful and rich, but the world doesn't revolve around you. This is a great running trail. If you'll notice, there are other people here, too."

"Yes, and if you'll notice, they're with me. I'm training them," she said, unable to conceal a touch of pride.

"For what?"

"What business is it of yours?"

"It's not. Just making conversation."

Ooooh, he was so exasperating!

"If you must know, we're training for a half-marathon," she said, lifting her chin an inch.

"Pretty impressive. You ever run a half?"

"Have you?" she threw back.

"I've run four wholes. I guess that would equal eight halves." The playful grin again.

"Full of yourself, aren't you?"

Was the man's sole purpose in life to annoy her?

"For what?" he asked then.

"What do you mean, for what?"

"What're you running for? What's the cause? If there's a team, there's always a cause. An organization. An event. A disease."

"The McDaniel Foundation."

What was she doing, still conversing with him? She should've cut him off a block ago.

"Ah."

Char said a prayer that the earth would suddenly open up and swallow Ryder McBride whole. Everywhere he went, he created a distraction. Her team members were beginning to glance back over their shoulders. Did they recognize him dressed the way he was, in running shorts, Ray-Bans, and a ball cap?

There was a brief silence in which all they could hear was the slap of their soles on the blacktop and each other's fast breathing, and then her curiosity overcame her common sense.

"What about you? You do this every Saturday morning?" She'd never seen him before on her regular route.

"Today's just a junk run. Did my LSD yesterday"—he interrupted himself—"you know, long slow distance."

She made a face. "I know what LSD means."

Unfazed, he went on. "But this is my first Saturday out here since I moved back. I've got a place in LA, but I'm working on a new project up here in Napa, and I need to get in shape for it. I'm living at my mom's for the summer."

He looked her way and grinned fetchingly.

Again.

Char wiped the perspiration off her forehead with her arm.

He knew full well that he was already "in shape." In fact, she couldn't imagine any way he could possibly be *more* in shape.

And then, Char's nerves got the best of her, and she began to giggle.

Oh, how she hated herself for letting him get to her, but she couldn't help it. Her giggle gurgled into a full-out laugh, and she lost her momentum.

Ryder slowed, too.

"What's the matter? You don't think I have it in me?"

Why, oh why, could she not wipe the stupid smile from her face?

"Obviously, you are fishing for compliments."

"Well, you might be right. Maybe I am. But I wouldn't do that if I didn't like you. I wouldn't care what you thought of me."

There was another lull as she tried to think of a smart retort, but then he saved her.

"Like I tried to say before, I'm sorry. For kissing you, I mean."

And then Ryder stopped, right there in the middle of the sidewalk, and stuck out his right hand.

It was that ancient gesture of trust, and Char, with her boarding school manners, responded instinctively with her own hand.

But recalling last night, she withdrew it just as swiftly.

Yet he was faster. He'd caught her before she could pull all the way back.

He was about to do it again. He reeled her body toward him, and as he did, a thrill shot through her, in spite of herself.

But unlike last night, when he'd rendered her gasping for air, this time both their chests were already heaving from the last half hour spent pounding the pavement.

Ryder wound her forearm into his side, drawing her so close she could feel his breath on her face. It held a trace of cinnamon toast.

He held her there, staring hard into her eyes while she anticipated a repeat of last night's performance. Then his gaze traveled down to her lips, and she braced herself for their onslaught. She gulped. Some primal emotion swept across his face; something dark enough to scare her, yet sweet enough to melt her fear.

And then, abruptly, he released her.

"Friends?" he asked cheerily.

"Friends," she echoed, because what else could she say? She'd be damned if she let him know he'd flustered her.

"Good," he said. He sprang away at a diagonal.

"Nice seeing you again. But I'll never get buff at this pace. Got to pick it up a little." He flashed her one last toothpaste-commercial smile.

Damn him! Every time she thought she "got" him, he proved her dead wrong. Now he'd left her discomfited all over again. She should be grateful he hadn't kissed her, but to her chagrin, disappointment swelled through her.

Lengthening his stride, he sprinted easily around Char and her pack, and in no time at all was far out in front.

Char watched his back—and his quads, biceps, and glutes—until he made a turn, taking him out of sight.

He'd definitely been coasting earlier, staying at her pace just so they could talk.

Char had been athletic all her life. She knew another jock when she saw one; she'd hate to be in competition with the likes of him. For the half-marathon, or any aspect of the challenge.

Not only would Ryder McBride have a good chance of actually winning a half-marathon purse himself, she could only imagine the auction items he could persuade people to donate to his cause, just because of who he was.

Luckily for her, he wasn't any part of the challenge.

A woman up ahead, eyes sparkling with mischief, called out, "Who was *that*?"

"Nobody," Char replied, thankful that Ryder wasn't quite so famous that he was immediately recognizable in running gear.

Yet.

"Four-mile mark!" she called out to her team, suppressing an inner smile.

Chapter 10

The e-mail was addressed to "R. McBride, President, NoCal Firefighters' Relief Fund."

The McDaniel Foundation is in receipt of your agency's application to participate in the Napa Charity Challenge, the valley's foremost charitable event.

He skimmed the details yet again. The run, the auction, and the gala.

Was he ready for this?

Ryder leaned back in his dad's creaky old desk chair, made a pyramid with his pointer fingers, and considered.

Could he pull it off?

Please stop by the foundation's office at your earliest convenience to pick up your materials. These include individual entry forms, donor forms, promotional items, and race jerseys.

It hadn't been very long since he'd taken the temporary reins of the FRF. Before that, it had been floundering on the brink of insolvency.

Joe, the FRF treasurer and a running buddy from way back, had been the first to feel him out about the situation. Joe knew that Ryder would be in town all summer. And he knew he was already a dedicated runner.

Then when the board of directors—most of them old friends of his dad—came and begged him for help with the challenge, he'd had no choice but to say yes.

They wanted to use him for his name and face. *Just one summer,* they'd said. *While you're up here filming. You'll just be a figurehead, really. The "interim president." We'll do all the heavy lifting.*

But Ryder had reasons of his own for wanting to help the Firefighters' Relief Fund.

Ever since the night seven years ago that had ripped life, as he knew it, out from under him.

It had begun with the midnight blare of a siren, jarring Ryder from a dead sleep.

He and his younger siblings were used to their father dropping everything when the alarm went off down at the firehouse. They knew the drill by heart. Dad would dash out to the garage to snatch the Nomex jacket with the bright yellow reflective stripes from its special peg.

Then, if the siren had interrupted supper or their homework, the kids would fly to the picture window to watch him throw his gear into the bed of his pickup and back out of the driveway with controlled urgency, the strip of red lights flashing on before he was past the big sycamore at the edge of the yard.

But whenever the alarm went off in the middle of the night, the kids turned over and went back to sleep.

They knew fighting fires was dangerous, of course. Apart from the obvious, they knew from what Dad and Mom always called to each other as the screen door slammed behind him.

"Love you."

"Love you too."

They didn't say that whenever one went out to the store or a ball game.

Still, to the kids, the danger was an abstract concept. Like the potential for blindness from running with a stick, something awful could happen, but it never did. Up until that night, Dad always came home from a fire—eventually.

* * *

Ryder was jarred from his thoughts by a light rap on the door of the study.

His mom materialized. She went over to the couch, leaned against its back, and studied the faded pattern on the carpet while she fiddled with the cross around her neck. Ryder tried to be patient while she chose her words.

"Bridget doesn't understand all this nonsense yet."

Ryder opened his mouth to reply, but she held up a silencing palm.

"Now, don't get me wrong; this isn't me scolding you. I'm fully aware that it's been your acting jobs that have got us through the past three years. If it weren't for you quitting college to pay our bills, I don't know where we'd be now. Probably in some government-subsidized apartment complex."

"Mom, cut it out. You know I quit school because I wanted to help. It wasn't a hard decision."

"I know. You were always that type of boy—responsible and a hard worker. Your brothers and sister and I will always be grateful for what you've done for us, since Dad died. So far, you've been a fine example for them."

Ryder's brows knit and unknit.

"So far?"

"Up till now, your acting has been like any other job. You have an apartment in LA. You go to work, you come visit us when you can—like any other big brother."

"Sure, we knew you were making a movie, but you weren't . . ." She hesitated. "Well, there's no better word for it: *famous*. Lately, people I haven't spoken to in years are asking about all these stories in the press.

"And at school, Bridget's friends are talking. You know how kids are today, exposed to stuff at a young age. Way too young."

She walked to the window, and Ryder twirled his pen.

"Even when *First Responder* became a hit, it was fine, for a while. But these publicity stunts are another thing. They're putting out a picture of my son that isn't very flattering."

Ryder shut the top of his laptop with a snap and gave his mom his full attention.

"Mom, I don't like it any more than you do. But it's not a big deal, so please don't take it so personally. That studio's paying Gould Entertainment big bucks to promote me. Believe me, it's the same with all actors who've reached a certain level of success."

"I'm no expert on the film business," said his mother. "It makes sense to me that you need publicity. All I'm saying is, I hope you won't let it get out of hand. Those girls from down in Hollywood you were photographed with last month. I know those were just party girls . . . women who get a kick out of the attention or like the money—"

"They're called 'MAWs,' Mom," Ryder interrupted. " 'Models/Actresses/Whatevers.' And believe me, they have no problem with being the object of attention. In fact, it's what they live for."

"*Whatever.* I'm not up on these things. But Chardonnay St. Pierre . . . that's something entirely different."

Her chin dipped down and to the right, and she eyed him sideways, in a version of her vast repertoire of mom-looks. Since he'd begun studying drama, Ryder had gained a new appreciation of just how skillfully she wielded her facial expressions. Maybe that's where his own acting ability had come from.

Hiding his bemusement, he mustered some polite patience.

"Okay, what's different about it?"

"This is Napa Valley, Ryder, not Los Angeles. I grew up in this county. Around here, everybody knows about the St. Pierres. Those girls go to our church!"

Of course, Ryder had heard of Domaine St. Pierre, but to him, it was just another winery. He could cite a dozen of them without even trying. The whole valley consisted of one vineyard after the other, lining both sides of narrow Highway 29, from Napa city in the south to Calistoga in the north.

"Think back; you've seen them. Don't you remember? When Saint Joan's is filled to bursting on Christmas and Easter, it's not just because of the occasion. Some of those people are there just to catch a glimpse of Chardonnay, Sauvignon, and Merlot St. Pierre, home for the holidays. It's no wonder. All three of them got their mother's looks and that French sense of style."

"Why," she said, chuckling in spite of herself, "I've heard Saint Joan's has gotten converts to Catholicism, just so that people could say they belong to the same church as the St. Pierres. Not that Father Ed minds. A convert is a convert."

She walked back over to the couch.

"Of course, you'll never see the great Xavier St. Pierre at mass with his girls. He was always too preoccupied with making wine and money—that is, when he was home at all," she added, her tone heavy with disapproval.

Ryder supposed that as a kid, he'd been more interested in baseball and bike riding than people watching. But if he'd ever seen Chardonnay before, he thought he'd have noticed.

"What about their mother?" asked Ryder. "Does she go to church with them?"

"You really don't know?" The expression she gave Ryder made him feel like a complete social derelict.

He responded with an empty look and a shrug.

"Lily d'Amboise, the actress! The one who ran off with that Argentine winemaker and got herself killed."

Chardonnay's mom was Lily d'Amboise?

Chardonnay's mom was dead?

"Tsk." His mom shook her head. "Such a tragedy for those little girls . . . motherless at ages eight, ten, and twelve. It was all the papers wrote about for days. Right afterward, Xavier packed them off to separate boarding schools back east. They only came home during the holidays and summers."

"Man, must've been hard. First their mom dies, then they get sent away. What happened after high school? They go to college?"

"The oldest one did. Even graduated law school. And Chardonnay won an athletic scholarship to UConn. There was a big fuss about that—the naysayers in town said it wasn't fair that a girl who could afford any college she wanted got a free ride. But after all, she did captain her prep school field hockey team to a championship.

"I heard the baby—'course, she's in her twenties now—the one who was in art school, recently dropped out."

She turned to the window, and Ryder peered past her, toward the furrowed hills.

"This is a small town, Ryder. People talk."

He'd had no idea that the St. Pierre girls were so idolized.

"My point is this. Chardonnay St. Pierre may seem like nothing but a spoiled rich girl on the surface. But she's had a rough go of it. Lost a parent at a young age. In that way, she's like you. She can't be enjoying this type of publicity."

Ryder made a skeptical face. "Seriously, Mom? That family goes out of its way to snag PR. St. Pierre practically begs for it with those big bashes he throws. He has his own publicist! Well, technically, it's the winery publicist, but you get my point. How do you think Amy got me into that party?"

"Don't lump the girls together with their father. He's notorious for his escapades. The police have been called out there I don't know how many times . . . breaking up fights, noise complaints. Do you know, he was arrested just yesterday for shooting a gun on his property?"

Belatedly, Ryder recalled Miranda's pronouncement at the table that had left Char red-faced. The night's later events had eclipsed that awkward moment.

"It's funny, but the daughters always seemed to be more mature than their parents. Chardonnay, in particular. She's well-known for her generosity. Volunteered in a couple of different places, including down at church. Like you, with your Firefighters' Relief Fund. Because of all that, there's a lot of empathy for her—and her sisters—around the valley."

She came over and perched on the edge of his desk.

"Her situation's not exactly like yours, of course. You've both had advantages, too, but in different ways. Char had money. But you had moral guidance."

Ryder stood.

"Call me dense, but I don't have any recollection of Char or her sisters."

"It's not all that surprising. You were always preoccupied with your sports and clubs and schoolwork. Like I said, they've been away for years. And you've been gone a while, too."

Ryder curled his arms around his petite mother and looked down on her brunette head that was showing a few faint wisps of silver. "Don't worry, I won't let the PR get too out of hand."

"I'm not worried. Just a little concerned."

She tilted her head back and kissed him on the chin.

"You're a good boy. A good man. I just have to get used to my son being a celebrity." She smiled wistfully.

When she'd gone, Ryder sank back down behind his computer screen, staring without seeing.

In addition to all the other worthy entities vying in the challenge, he was about to set himself up against Chardonnay St. Pierre's.

She'd been all he could think about during the remainder of his morning run and in the car driving home. He'd already registered his organization, and now his mom tells him that Char and her sisters were also the darlings of the valley.

Naturally, she would have connections. Big-time connections. Other wineries, growers, fancy eateries, old-money families. And she'd be a fool not to use them.

All that on top of being gorgeous and athletic.

Could he compete with that?

What the hell had he gotten himself into?

But then, in his mind's eye, he saw again the stricken faces of his mother, brothers, and sister when the chief had knocked on their front door that dusty August dawn . . . helmet in hand, his wife and other crew wives standing solemnly behind him, toting the telltale casseroles.

He saw again the dark splotches of his mother's tears on his father's flag-draped casket. The growing stack of bills in the basket on Dad's desk—the very desk he now sat behind.

Today that basket was empty, thanks to Amy's improbable discovery of him as he knelt in a candlelit church.

If there was any way in hell he could help another family going through that kind of pain, he would.

Whatever Chardonnay's pretty little charity was, he figured his was more important. At least, it was to him and other fire victims.

Besides, Ryder brightened, he had certain advantages, too.

He looked at his calendar. He'd been running since high school; he'd merely tweaked his routine to prep for the half. He had a ready-made team in his band of brothers in the FRF.

Shooting didn't start until July, giving him a month to up his reps and weights and study his lines at night, and find them a building to work out of. That had been Ryder's idea. Once he moved back down to LA in the fall, he wanted to leave behind a legacy—a headquarters for the organization.

He scribbled a note across the "Monday" square on the broad, old-fashioned desk-blotter calendar. *McD Fdtn—pick up stuff for challenge.*

Then he went outside and mowed his mother's lawn.

Chapter 11

Sunday, June 15

"And today's attendance is seventy-two," announced Father Ed.

Chardonnay fidgeted in her pew, hyperaware of the eyes trained on her every move. She glanced sideways as discreetly as possible. *And fifty of them are crowded around us.* How could Meri and Savvy sit there so serenely?

It was always this way the first Sunday they came home in the summer and on holidays. It unnerved Char sometimes. How on earth did the word get out? Being gawked at in the shops and on the streets just because she was the daughter of a famous—rather, infamous—vintner made her feel uneasy. Undeserving.

But even with the stares, she'd always found solace at the little adobe church.

Of the three, Char was the seeker. Meri was absorbed in her art, and Savvy had chosen the law as her guide to life. Yet they all found common ground in the observance of mass. Its tradition provided a comfortable structure that they were missing in their broken home. Char never had to coerce the others into going. Following months apart at their respective schools, it was a ritual that teased them back into something almost like a legitimate family unit.

If not for the devout French au pair who'd first brought the girls here as toddlers, they'd never have discovered Saint Joan's; no one else in their family was remotely spiritual. Cousin Patrick was serving time for dealing coke. Another cousin, Paul—though only thirty—had already spent his way through a fortune and now preyed on rich, married women. And Uncle Phil had an upcoming court date for tax evasion.

As far as Char remembered, the only time Papa had ever gone to church was to attend his wife's funeral. Neither he nor Maman had ever talked to the girls about God or religion or the concept of giving something back of their tremendous fortune.

Then, as now, Papa was always either working, partying, or traveling. His absences were the norm. In fact, it was a novelty when he showed up for a weekday meal.

But Char, unlike Papa, was home to stay. She couldn't wait for the day when she could walk into mass without any fanfare whatsoever.

Ryder sat with his family toward the right rear of the church. He tried to pay attention to the priest, but his eyes, like everybody else's, kept wandering to the beauties up front and left.

Bridget followed his line of sight. Leave it to her to never miss a trick.

"Who are they?" she whispered loudly into Ryder's ear.

"Who?" Ryder feigned ignorance.

"Those girls everyone's looking at," she hissed.

Thankfully, Mom's "shhh" lips put a lid on Bridget's questions for the moment.

During the sermon when there was a break from the rhythm of kneeling and standing, Ryder studied the St. Pierres from his rear pew. Only very recently, down in LA, had he ever known people who had what they called in the business "star power." Like the rare actor, those three girls also possessed that indescribable "it" quality—whatever "it" was. Must be genetic. With no apparent effort, they exuded some magnetic, unself-conscious cool. What was it about them? The only answer was *everything*. From the way their long hair curved around their slim shoulders and how the simple lines of their clothes skimmed their bodies, to the identical tilt of their heads when they talked and the intoxicating scent of flowers that hung in the air around them. It would be easy to explain away as the smell of money. But lately, he'd brushed shoulders with enough women with similar trappings—absent the class—to recognize true chic when he was in its presence.

"We look for the resurrection of the dead, and the life of the world to come. Amen," intoned the priest.

Inexplicably, at that moment Chardonnay's head swiveled and her eyes caught Ryder's.

His totally unprepared heart cartwheeled. Had she *felt* his eyes caressing her?

Recognition flashed warmly on her face, curving her lips up a centimeter before she turned back around.

The whole thing had taken two seconds, but to Ryder it eclipsed his whole morning.

Over his sister's head, his mom gave him a dark, warning look. Maternal overprotectiveness. It'd gotten more intense after Dad died. He supposed it had something to do with shouldering the entire weight of raising four kids all by herself. He and Bridget and the twins were pretty good at tolerating it. Fortunately, neither he nor his siblings were prone to troublemaking. That would've pushed Mom over the brink.

When the last hymn closed, the way his mom herded her brood out of the building would've put a border collie to shame.

"Jeez, Mom!" complained Bridget, twisting her neck backward as her mother planted a fingertip between her shoulder blades and nudged. "What's the rush? I wanted to look at those girls some. Hey! One of them looks just like the girl in the picture with Ryder . . ."

"Don't stare, Bridget. Let's give them their privacy. For heaven's sake, this is mass, not a fashion show."

Ryder turned wistfully too, trying to come up with a good-enough reason to lag behind and talk to Char, but the St. Pierres were now surrounded by a knot of people. Besides, there was his family to consider. Ben and Brian had bolted out the double doors ahead of them, and his mother was ready to go. Opportunity lost.

* * *

For a quarter of an hour, Char and her sisters were held up in the sanctuary, cornered by parishioners who wanted a word. Some were genuine friends, anxious to welcome them home. A few were brazen enough to introduce themselves for the first time. All were on their best behavior, and there was no good excuse not to be gracious.

Finally, Father Eduardo, his tummy nicely disguised by his white robes, took Char's elbow.

"Excuse us, will you?" Miraculously parting the hangers-on, he guided her toward an interior door.

Savvy peered over the heads of the throng that had swallowed her up, and Char wiggled her fingers good-bye.

"Thank you," Char whispered to Father Ed as they made their way down the familiar rubber-treaded steps leading to the church basement.

"Welcome home," he said. "And congratulations on your degree. Public policy, isn't it?"

Char smiled, pleased he'd remembered. She'd be willing to bet that Papa didn't know what subject she'd majored in. "Mm-hm. How are donations these days?"

"Up, I'm happy to say. Spring cleaning, you know. We must have a dozen trash bags full of clothing that needs sorted."

They'd come to a room lined with shelves full of odds and ends: a toaster, lamps, some mismatched dishes. The floor was stacked with plastic storage bins, their lids marked with sizes.

"Our usual deal? I help sort, in exchange for a few bins for my friends?"

Father nodded. "Fine by me. I took a cursory glance—mostly outgrown school clothes, still in good shape."

Char opened a bag and pulled out a wrinkled, child-sized shirt, then dropped it back in.

"I think I'll go ahead and sort these now. I told Meri and Savvy I might stay after to do donations. We drove separately."

"Suit yourself. The sooner they get sorted, the sooner they'll be available for distribution."

While her sisters drove home, Char dove into the bags, distributing the items into the appropriate bins. For the hundredth time, she thought back to freshman winter break, when she'd gone home with a friend whose parents taught her the meaning of the term "noblesse oblige."

Like Char's family, Candy Golberg's parents were well off. They had the big glass and steel contemporary in Chicago, the sprawling A-frame in Vail they called the cabin, and the "cottage"—the ginger-bread Victorian on the shore of Lake Michigan. But unlike Maman and Papa, the Golbergs made it their policy to give back. Dr. Golberg spent every January in Honduras operating on children's cleft palates, free of charge. Char had seen pictures; it was no picnic. He lived in a tent, paid his own airfare, and came back covered with mosquito bites.

Mrs. Golberg sat on several boards and ran the daycare at the Y in one of Chicago's poorer neighborhoods, donating back her small salary. Every Christmas she hauled her kids to the soup kitchen to serve up meals. They were used to it, even made an event of it, laughing and talk-ing with the regular "customers." And if the Golbergs happened to have company for the holidays, guess what? *They* went, too.

Mrs. Golberg said, "I always told my kids: What you do with your money tells as much about you as how you earned it—if not more."

Candy was no slouch back at Hollyhurst Academy, either. On their free days, when they had no schoolwork between breakfast and evening vespers, she volunteered at a local nursing home. Char even went with her a couple of times.

Char never forgot that. From then on, she made it her mission to help out whenever and wherever she could.

Helping others—in any capacity—never failed to warm her heart. But when she started focusing in on migrant kids, she knew she'd found her true passion. Those kids couldn't help where they were born or that their parents didn't speak English. Here were people who put her own problems into perspective. This wasn't just random char-ity. This was her raison d'être. Her life's work.

Happiness spread through her as she anticipated the looks on the children's faces when she distributed the clean, good quality clothes, over on El Valle Avenue. It always took a few weeks until people caught on to the fact that she was there on summer Wednesdays.

That's why it was so important that she establish a permanent, year-round identity.

She was dying to get inside that building, to check on the layout. She'd been making notes of her questions as they came to mind, and now they filled up several pages. Only three more days till her next appointment with Bill Diamond.

Chapter 12

"Remember, no canvassing until Saturday! The rules only allow a two-week period to collect donations."

"I remember," called Char.

Following her meeting at the McDaniel Foundation, Char closed Nicole Simon's office door behind her, juggling her heavy cardboard box full of challenge paraphernalia.

Yay! The long-awaited event was finally here.

Her first official task was to find donors of auction items for the gala, and in her head, she was already listing prospects—even if she couldn't actually contact anyone yet.

Her mind was racing with the restaurants she'd ask to donate dinner certificates, spas that might contribute treatments, and wineries that could offer free tours.

She knew of several farm markets that could be persuaded to provide baskets of produce, and she visualized how colorful they'd look, wrapped up in ribbons on the auction tables at the culminating gala. Attractive donations like that would be sure to draw bids.

But timing was key. She had to get to the big donors first or risk losing out to the other competitors. She could hardly wait to rush home and prioritize her list of contacts.

She crossed the reception area and was in the midst of squeezing herself, her handbag, and the cardboard carton through the exterior door, when deep within her bag her phone rang.

With difficulty, Char freed up one hand and dug for it.

Its display said "County of Napa." *Commissioner Jones.* She'd been waiting for this.

But as she raised her cell to her ear, the box slipped through her arms, sending papers, jerseys, brochures, and pens tumbling down the concrete steps.

Worse, trying to salvage one particularly thick file that was about to spill, Char dropped her phone. The sickening clatter as it bounced down the steps made her wince as she foresaw the hassle of getting a new one. There went the whole afternoon. If she hadn't been in such a god-awful hurry . . .

To make matters worse, who should be strolling across the street but Ryder McBride.

"Let me help." He jogged toward her, retrieving some papers off the sidewalk.

Char scooped her phone from the ground. The screen was blank. She hit some buttons. *Nada.*

Ryder eyed her with concern.

"Is it okay?"

"The screen's blank."

He reached for it. She hesitated, then handed it over. While he busied himself over it, she lowered herself to the ground to scoop up the rest of her papers.

But a frisson of suspicion settled on her. Because nothing was simple when it came to Ryder McBride.

"What brings you downtown?" she asked.

Ryder's attention was still focused on her phone.

Char peered up at him from where her hands and knees were planted on the rough pavement. A strolling couple stepped out of their way to avoid her, then tittered over her awkward position.

"Same thing that brought you here, by the looks of things," he replied, still absorbed.

Her skepticism mounted.

"I'm here to pick up my stuff for the Napa Charity Challenge. Where are you going?" she said, her wariness unavoidably creeping into her voice. The McDaniel offices were on a commercial street, next to some other small businesses. He could be headed to any one of them. All the same, a bud of dread unfurled in the pit of her stomach.

Ryder smiled then and gestured with her phone toward the door she'd just come out of.

"Like I said, same thing."

A gust of wind sent a brochure fluttering down the street, and he lunged for it.

Char's mind spun as she began to piece together the puzzle.

He'd been interested in Nicole Simon last Friday night at the party.

He knew a lot about local government statistics and underserved members of society.

And—*uh-oh*—only serious runners did junk runs.

Please, god, no. The bud of dread sprouted a leaf.

But Ryder couldn't possibly be participating in the challenge. He was nothing but an actor. A self-serving, publicity-seeking actor. They were all the same.

Through the doorway of the foundation, out stepped Nicole Simon, brow furrowed.

"Chardonnay! I saw you drop your box from out my window! Are you all right?

Greaaaaaaat. Pasting on a smile, Char scrambled to her feet.

"I'm fine," she said breezily, brushing dirt off her knees. "I've got it under control."

"Is your phone broken?" Dr. Simon asked.

"Nope, it's fixed," said Ryder, handing it back.

Char squinted in the bright sunlight. Her familiar screen saver blinked on.

"Thanks," she said, surprised by both his kindness and his knack for technology.

In the awkward moment that followed, as she checked to see if the commissioner had left a message, Dr. Simon cleared her throat, and Char looked up.

The professor had a youthful twinkle in her eye.

So that's why she'd come to the doorway. She'd seen Ryder from her window, and she was waiting for an introduction.

"Dr. Simon, I'd like you to meet Ryder McBride. Ryder, Dr. Nicole Simon, chair of the McDaniel Foundation."

The doctor extended her hand and smiled like she was sixteen again and Ryder had just showed up in a convertible to take her to the prom.

Ryder took her hand in both of his.

"I've been looking forward to meeting you for years."

Huh? Only seconds after he'd impressed her with his tech skills, he was showing his true Hollywood stripes again, sucking up to Nicole Simon?

Char looked from one to the other and back again.

"Oh?" Dr. Simon all but swooned, right there on the stairs. "Now, how could that possibly be?"

"I was once registered to take your class at San Jose State—before I had to take a leave of absence," said Ryder.

"You don't say!" Dr. Simon's hand fluttered to her breast. "You were a student at San Jose?"

Ryder grinned and lowered his eyes modestly. "It was three years ago, before I started acting. You were the most popular professor on campus, and your course in economy and sociology had finally opened up."

Then, before she could reply, he changed the subject.

"I was just on my way in to see you, to pick up my materials for the challenge."

"Pardon me?" Dr. Simon looked confused.

And all at once, her whole face lit up.

"Why, you must be R. McBride! President of the Firefighters' Relief Fund! Of course! You'll forgive me for not making the connection earlier. I noticed you just the other night at Chardonnay's affair and had so hoped to make your acquaintance, but there were so many people bothering you already, and I didn't want to be too forward . . ."

Graciously, Ryder extended his arm toward the door to indicate that Dr. Simon should precede him inside, and then he followed.

"Well, this is very exciting! *The* Ryder McBride, a participant in the challenge . . ."

Their voices trailed away as the two disappeared back inside the office.

Caught up in their mutual admiration, they had left Char standing alone on the sidewalk, evidently forgotten.

The nerve of Ryder McBride!

The man was a walking, talking roller-coaster ride. She'd been wary at their introduction. Inflamed by his kiss. Indignant at the photograph. Giggly at seeing him on the run . . . even disappointed that he hadn't kissed her again. And now, again, she was so furious she could spit.

She didn't know what to react to first—or rather, next: that Ryder had just upstaged her with the very woman she wanted as her advisor, or the fact that he was about to become her biggest competitor in the first public endeavor of her professional life.

How was it that a man she'd first set eyes on only three days ago could be turning her world upside down?

Char used a knee to boost up the heavy box again, lugged everything to her car, and called back Commissioner Jones. Who confirmed the stats Ryder had tossed off Friday night. Apparently, Ryder really knew his stuff.

Char pulled out of her parking spot. She had a lot to think about.

She headed north toward home, not seeing the vine-covered ridges and pale yellow mustard plants combing the valley on both sides of the two-lane highway.

How did Ryder McBride know so much about orphans? Why would an actor give two hoots about demographics?

He'd mentioned taking classes at San Jose State in . . . what was it he'd said? Economics and sociology?

And what on earth was the Firefighters' Relief Fund? Had Char heard Dr. Simon right—that Ryder was its president?

Who exactly *was* Ryder McBride anyway?

Chapter 13

In the afternoon, Char drove to a neighborhood far away from the touristy areas of the valley. The enticing aromas of cumin and oregano hit her as she got out of her car.

A little girl of nine or so waved to her from the porch steps of a modest home with a warped chain-link fence, across the street from the lot where Char parked.

She waved back, and soon the child's mother came out and watched Char set up a small folding table and begin emptying her boxes of donated clothes onto it.

"*¡Hola, Amelia, Juanita!*" called Char, waving. "Come over and say hi!"

They crossed the street, a shy younger boy in a white T-shirt lagging behind.

Char propped her hands on her hips and examined the girl.

"*¡Cómo has crecido!* Do you remember me from last summer?"

The girl's mother said something to her in Spanish.

Char only picked up the gist of the conversation. "I used to see you and Juan every week last summer. Your *madre* is the best cook! She used to bring me tamales all the time."

That jogged Amelia's memory, and she smiled bashfully, then hugged her mother's legs through her skirt.

Juanita's wet brown eyes met Char's in a meaningful gaze that didn't need any translation. Juanita was a widow. Her husband, a picker, had died when Juan was just a baby. Both women knew that Juanita hadn't started bringing Char her Mexican soul food specialties just for the heck of it. It was a proud woman's way of repaying Char for her weekly donations of food and toys—and sometimes plain old cash.

That's when Char had made up her mind which of her many causes moved her the most.

Char peered around Juanita's womanly form. "It's nice to see you, too, Juan. Hey, you like Levi's? I hope so, because I have a whole pile of them here that I don't know what to do with. I only guessed at sizes; I haven't seen you in a whole year!"

Juan's eyes lit up as he reached tentatively for the shopping bag Char held out. She'd topped it off with new socks and pajamas from the mall.

"And here's yours." Char handed another bag to Amelia.

"What are you cooking over there, Juanita? I could smell it the minute I opened my car door."

"*Nacatamales.* Like in the Michoacán. I give you some next week. You coming back?"

"I'll be here. Every Wednesday. From now on."

"You done with college?"

"Uh-huh. I'm home to stay."

Juanita's genuine smile warmed Char to her soul. This was what she wanted. To be home and to be of service.

"Juanita, who owns this building?"

She shrugged. "Nobody. I wish somebody would do something with it. It's just a place for older kids to hang out, get in trouble. When you're not here, I keep my kids away."

More people were meandering up the street, some familiar, some not. It was the third year Char had been coming to the parking lot of the vacant building to distribute donations from church. Every year, more people came. And every year, the building fell deeper into disrepair.

But Char intended to change all that.

Minutes later, all heads turned when Bill Diamond's logo-splashed car pulled in.

Char was so antsy to get inside the door of the building she could hardly contain herself, watching him fumble among a dozen keys for the right one.

Suddenly an idea hit her.

"Juanita, come along."

"¿Cómo?"

"Will you join me?" She motioned with her arm. "C'mon. Bring the kids."

Juanita looked doubtful, but she gathered up Amelia and Juan, and together they moved toward the door.

"Anxious to see the place, aren't you?" asked Bill, perplexed. "Well, don't get too excited. It's nothing like the spread you got up there on Dry Creek Road."

He handed her a key. "Here, I'll let you do the honors."

He couldn't have been more right. The few bare lightbulbs that worked barely lit up the interior. Probably a blessing, since what Char could see was filthy. There were beverage cans tossed around on the floors and junk piled up in the corners.

"Squatters," said Bill. He went over and kicked a can, scattering dust motes. "Long gone now."

But the floors were wood, and the raggedy roller blinds camouflaged tall windows. Char yanked on one, and it made a racket snapping all the way up, sending years' worth of dust into the air.

She turned to Bill. "I love it! It's perfect!"

Juanita looked at her like she was *loco*. Little Juan ventured a few feet away to go exploring.

"¡Juan Garza!" His mother let loose with a torrent of Spanish, bringing him scurrying back to her side.

"Isn't this cool?" asked Char. She approached one of the longer walls. "Picture this, Juanita. A little cantina with a counter where you could do your cooking!"

Now Juanita really looked nervous.

"Think of it! With your culinary talent, you could pack 'em in. Just do a limited menu, be open a few days a week. The kids could hang out right here, under your supervision." She smiled encouragingly, and slowly Juanita began to get it.

"I don't know. Mayyyybeee," she said, looking around with new eyes.

"You could make tamales, *corundas*," said Char, citing some of her favorite dishes.

"Is hard to find *charanda* around here," said Juanita. "We could sell that, too."

"Now you're talking!"

Bill raised his eyebrows. "Don't you want to know what the asking price is?"

"Oh," Char said. "Yes. What is the asking price?"

"Three hundred thousand."

Char's smile faded. She looked around again, more critically this time.

"C'mon, I'll walk you through," said Bill.

But the more she saw of it, the more she was sure.

Then she remembered her most important question.

"Tell me something. Are you helping Ryder McBride buy this?" she asked.

"Like I said before, I'm working for the seller. I'll show the property to anyone who expresses an interest. First come, first serve. That said, it wouldn't be appropriate for me to comment on other potential buyers. Or"—he added with a meaningful look—"any offers they might have made."

Damn. She wanted this building. But where was she going to get three hundred thousand dollars on her own?

Chapter 14

Ryder McBride would be practically unrecognizable in his fireman's helmet and bunker gear—a fact that wasn't lost on him.

After memorizing his lines, he'd stayed up late last night, strategizing. Listing potential contributors, mapping them out for his team. Chardonnay St. Pierre probably knew every hotshot in the valley. All the big winery owners, for sure, and lots of other businesspeople.

But that wasn't the worst thing. The hell with begging for donations from other people. Char's old man could annihilate all her competition with one big fat check.

Ryder slumped back in his desk chair, reality closing in before he'd even got started. His team could work twenty-four-seven for the next two weeks, and Char could still win.

He recalled yet again his mother's dire straits following his dad's death.

And more recently, poor Lori MacKenzie raising two kids on a cashier's salary. Only a year ago, Lori's husband James had died in a wreck between the pumper he was helming and some crazy-ass civilian in a jacked-up sports car.

Ryder's body sat motionless as his mind raced. There had to be a way to beat Team Char.

Then he remembered. All the team captains had been advised never to reveal how much they'd raised at any point in the campaign. In the past, near winners had been overheard bragging about their war chests, only to be outdone when a competitor went running to a big corporate sponsor who'd written a single check on the spot.

If Chardonnay didn't know how much her competition raised, she wouldn't know how much she had to raise to beat them.

She wouldn't expect much out of a small outfit like his. But then, she had no idea how much the FRF meant to him and the rest of the department.

His best bet was to work like a dog and downplay his progress. It wouldn't be the first time David beat Goliath.

Plus, he brightened as he remembered that Char was just as green at this as he was. She was no experienced fund-raiser. Just a wine princess. He started writing, and within a half hour, he had a fresh plan.

His mission: to outdo Chardonnay in contributions for the auction. His tactic: to mount an organized attack on small-time donors.

If she had the valley's elite sewn up, he would go after the regular folks. Since each of his donations would probably be smaller than hers, he'd have to get more of them, which meant covering more ground. Whatever. He might not have her contacts, but he had more endurance and dedication than a whole cellar full of wine princesses.

Chapter 15

Early the next morning, Ryder was eating breakfast at the diner with the other FRF board members. He waited until the others were immersed in typically rambunctious conversation to run an idea by his treasurer.

Lowering his voice a notch, he asked, "You know that empty commercial building I was telling you about over on El Valle? I think it would be great to use as an adjunct to the little station house we have. You know, so we don't have to meet in restaurants. Do some community outreach, maybe install some workout equipment."

Joe forked some eggs into his mouth.

"I don't know. I kinda like having meetings in restaurants."

Ryder ignored that. "I drove by it again yesterday. It's nothing fancy, but we don't need fancy. Just somewhere to put an office, some storage, and a gathering space. Maybe run some fire education programs for the neighborhood, too."

"Might be a good idea to recruit some young people. It's not in the best area of town, but if we got some student volunteers, it could be useful to them *and* us. Give the youth something constructive to do," said Joe.

Joe's initial comments were encouraging. If Ryder was going to make this happen, he needed board support.

"Exactly. Make them feel like they're part of the community."

"What're they asking?"

"I called the Realtor. Three hundred k. But they might come down. The guy said it's been empty for about three years."

"They could come down by half, and it still wouldn't be low enough. The way things stand, we couldn't even invest in a Porta-Potty."

"We could if someone on our team wins the half-marathon. That would give us a sweet little down payment."

The always levelheaded Joe grunted. "You're the only one who's fast enough to do that."

"What about Dan? Ever watch him run? He's got a pretty good kick, for an old-timer," said Ryder.

"Watch who you're calling old! 'Sides, he's only about forty, isn't he?"

"Hey"—Joe slapped Ryder good-naturedly with the back of his hand—"that reminds me. How come you're not taking advantage of your pretty face to collect donations? Hell, if I had the women crawling all over me, you wouldn't find this old boy with a helmet covering his head."

Ryder ducked his chin, embarrassed. "Aw, let me do it my way first. Besides, I think you're blowing this fame thing way out of proportion. I'm not that big of a deal."

"Ha," Joe exclaimed, draining his orange juice. " 'Not a big deal,' he says. Then why were the wife and her book club going all gaga last night when I mentioned I was meeting with you this morning? 'Course, they'd had a couple o' glasses of wine in them. . . ."

"How are the MacKenzies doing these days?" Ryder changed the subject.

"Doing good. Lori's still working at the market, and she got Jamie a summer job there, too."

"What about Jimmy?"

"FRF just got a thank-you note for the check we sent to cover his baseball camp."

"If we could buy that building, we could put in a rec room and a snack bar. Mentor kids like him. Kids who need some positive role models in their lives."

Ryder checked the time and slammed the rest of his coffee. He addressed his men. "Let's roll. Everyone'll be waiting."

A few miles away, at the little fire station off 29, Ryder scanned the room of volunteers squeezed into the foyer. Among them were his core group of FRF members, plus a cadre of reserve and career firefighters.

"Thanks for coming, everyone. Glad to see you brought your bunker gear. That'll come in handy when we're asking for funds. Luckily, it's not too hot out today. Use your boots to solicit on the street corners. Here are your maps and lists of contacts," he said, passing out papers.

"Remember, this is for the benefit of firefighters and other victims of fire throughout northern California. God forbid, someday the money we're raising may even help your own family or the family of the man or woman standing next to you.

"I'll start at the north end of the valley. Drop off everything you get—pledges, checks, whatever—at the nearest station. Dan, you take a team up to Calistoga. I'll follow you up, then work my way south and do pickups at the end of the day."

Char reread the instructions in the challenge pamphlet. *"The Mc-Daniel Foundation will grant one million dollars to the registered charity that raises the most money in the designated two-week period. Qualifying donations include outright monetary donations, plus bids placed at the gala on donated items during the final night of the competition.*

"A fifty-thousand-dollar bonus contribution will be granted to the charity of the one individual who wins the half-marathon.

"All charities are directed not to disclose the amount they have raised during the two-week period. The winner will be determined after bidding closes on the night of the gala. The totals will be calculated during dinner and dancing, and announced at the conclusion of the evening."

She set the instructions aside then and started writing down the names she'd been carrying in her head all semester. First she racked her brain for all the business owners she knew personally. Then she did some research online and added to her growing list. Unfamiliar businesses she assigned to her teammates.

Bright and early Saturday morning, she started making phone calls. But thirty minutes later, she was dissatisfied. She didn't have the personal cell numbers of several potentially prime donors, even though she'd known them casually for years . . . shopping at their stores, eating at their restaurants. Those were the same people who knew her immediately by sight and who were certain to help her cause if she showed up to see them in person.

Ordinarily, Char didn't take advantage of her celebrity. She tried to not even think about it until she was out and about and noticed that people were whispering—though most of the locals were pretty good about respecting her privacy, even if they did stare. But if flaunting her name and face could help some of those migrant kids . . .

She could simply start phoning business numbers, but she knew from her own family business that the employees who answered those phones were paid to be gatekeepers.

What's more, her own phone number was private. Harried business owners routinely ignored anonymous calls on their cells.

Leaving messages took too long. By the time people called her back, there was a good chance they would already have been hit up by somebody else. There wasn't time for e-mail, either. Not if she wanted to get to the key people first.

This was a job that had to be done in person.

There were dozens of stops to make and no time to lose. She was going to win this thing. It was her best chance for cementing a brand-new, squeaky clean reputation in the valley. But more than that, it was the best chance for nabbing that building for those kids.

She grabbed the list of names and arranged them in rough order by location. Then she took a fistful of fliers and tore out the door again.

Highway 29 had the greatest number of establishments, but there were some over-the-top places along the Silverado Trail where she knew people. She could head up the trail and later parallel back down the highway.

* * *

Char got lucky all morning. If anything, it'd been tough tearing herself away from people she hadn't seen for months . . . even years. Everyone knew Papa, some had even known Maman—or said that they had—and they all wanted a firsthand account of what Char and her sisters were up to. She tried to be gracious, giving pat answers while guarding her sisters' privacy. Most of her contacts were discreet, but some would be tweeting as she walked out their door, spreading Char's scant family news. "Sorry, but I have a lot of ground to cover. I have to keep moving" was the excuse she used over and over.

By the time she hit Calistoga, the front seat of her car was stacked to the window with sponsorships, pledges, and gift certificates.

As she pulled into the tiny northern town, the sound of sirens detracted from the chic shop windows and tree-lined sidewalks. Traffic was slowed to a standstill. She pulled over and parked in the first empty space. From there it would be an easy walk to virtually all the businesses in the square.

She'd passed only a couple of shops when the spectacle that had created the traffic jam became evident. A shiny yellow fire truck was parked in a vacant lot off the town's main intersection, lights flashing, siren blaring. Children were climbing in and out of it, supervised by their parents and some uniformed firemen. A van with a TV news logo, its satellite receiver ratcheted up, was pulled in next to it.

At all four corners of the little town's main intersection were Nomex-jacketed firefighters soliciting vehicles at stop signs. Hands waved dollar bills out car windows, depositing them in the boots held out by the firemen.

There was an especially big crowd—for Calistoga, anyway—around one tall figure. Char could just see his helmet above the others' heads.

She edged closer. In the center of the throng, thrusting a microphone into the man's face, Char recognized an attractive reporter from out of Santa Rosa. Calistoga was too small to have its own station.

She walked to the edge of the tightly packed throng to better hear what was being said.

"Folks," the reporter said to her cameraman, "in case you haven't been to the movies lately, this man dressed as a firefighter is none other than Napa's own Ryder McBride. Ryder's had great success with *First Responder*. Ryder, tell us what it is you're doing out here on the streets of Calistoga today."

"I'm here on behalf of my favorite cause, the Firefighters' Relief Fund. Every year, children and families struggle to recover from fires. Fires destroy our property and our lives. The Firefighters' Relief Fund of northern California provides assistance to those families."

He was a great interview—natural and yet professional. He knew how to divide his attention equally between the reporter and the cameraman.

"Ryder, I understand the FRF is one of the foundations taking part in this year's mega-fund-raiser, the Napa Charity Challenge, sponsored by the McDaniel Foundation?"

Someone jostled Char, forcing her a step backward. The movement attracted Ryder's eye. From that instant on, he managed to continue answering the rest of the reporter's questions with his usual charm, all the while maintaining steady eye contact with Char.

"... the real story, and that is, that you're actually an honest-to-goodness fireman?" the glamorous reporter asked.

"Haven't been able to volunteer down in Los Angeles. Work's kept me busy lately."

He displayed a blinding grin. The onlookers smiled and nodded at one another, eating it up, as the interview continued.

What timing he had. He knew exactly when to smile and when to appear serious. How to work the crowd and the reporter simultaneously. And to think, he was totally untrained. Or so the gossip said.

"Ryder, tell us what you're working on next."

Char watched, entranced. For once, she was the observer instead of the observed. Nobody paid the least bit of attention to her. All eyes were on Ryder.

True, back east, at school, she was an unknown—at least until people found out her name. But here in the valley, Char was used to being the center of attention. It gave her an odd sensation, being in the background for a change. Pleasant, but odd.

"I'm not here to talk about myself today. I'm here to bring attention to the needs of firefighters and their families . . ."

If she'd had a white flag, she'd have waved it. Curving her lips into a line that was half-smile, half-smirk, she shook her head at Ryder in tacit surrender, turned, and walked back to her car.

Ryder McBride had won the Battle of Calistoga today. Might as well head back south.

Was this how he was going to the play the game? Use his celebrity and dress up in a fireman's costume? He was going after the prize with double barrels. She'd better remember that.

Later that evening, when the sun was almost below the horizon, an exhausted Char dragged herself on weary legs into the kitchen.

Meri and Savvy swiveled on their stools at the granite counter where they were sipping wine and munching salads.

"Where have you been?" Savvy asked casually between bites.

"Out soliciting." Char exhaled heavily as she climbed onto a stool.

"How'd it go?" asked Meri.

"Pretty good, at first. I started out in Yountville—got everyone in our favorite spots. Oils and Almonds donated a humongous gift basket. Then I went along the Silverado Trail and hit up La Maison de la Lune. They gave me a weekend package for two."

"Sweet," said Savvy.

"I stopped at every vineyard and tasting room, all the way up to Calistoga. You'll never guess who I ran into there."

Char placed her hands on the counter and leaned forward for emphasis.

"Firefighters." She sat back to let that momentous news sink in.

"Firefighters?" repeated Meri, showing a disappointing lack of concern. She took a big bite of avocado.

"Firefighters! *In uniform.*"

"Was there a fire up in Calistoga?" asked Savvy.

Char sighed. Starting from the beginning, she filled them in on what she'd learned about Ryder McBride since last Friday night.

"And best of all," she said with a sarcastic grin, "guess who some

TV reporter was interviewing, right in the center of town? So it turns out, along with being Hollywood's darling, he's an athlete, a student of sociology, and president of some firefighters' organization. And he's got firemen soliciting donations for the challenge. You should've seen them, looking all hot in their yellow jackets, working the street corners, holding out their boots for dollar bills. And being pretty successful, from what I could see."

"Clever. Please pass the salt," said Savvy.

"Do you realize what this means?" Char exclaimed.

"I don't see how it's all that bad," said Meri.

"Are you kidding? Nothing could be worse!" Char said, exasperated. "What's hotter than a movie star?"

"Um . . . a movie star in a fireman's outfit?" asked Savvy.

"Exactly. Everybody loves firefighters. They're big and they're strong, and they save your house and rescue your kids and your dog. They're sexy, too. Why do you think they use them on calendars? Ryder's got a huge advantage in the challenge, right out of the gate."

"Is there any of that bread left from Bouchon?" asked Meri.

Char threw her hands in the air. How could she make them understand how Ryder had sabotaged her cause?

"Ryder might've gotten lots of small donations today. But I'll bet one vintner friend of Papa's can top that with one stroke of his pen," said Meri.

"Still, it's the publicity. He'll be the hot topic all over Calistoga tonight, and he'll be in the papers and online, too."

"That's pretty ironic, isn't it?" piped in Savvy. "Out of all of us, you're the one who's always hated attention the most. And now you're suddenly envious of Ryder's PR."

Char sighed, and then Savvy scowled.

"Wait a minute. You said there was a reporter up there?"

"Sylvia Chen from KEMO."

"How'd she know McBride would be in Calistoga today?"

Char paused and then it dawned on her. Ryder must've called the press, and then set up the whole colorful spectacle. The charming town square, the kiddie tours of the fire engine, and the rugged firefighters in uniform, holding out their boots.

"Never mind," said Savvy. "We're just getting started. Here"—she slid the wooden salad bowl across the table—"eat something. Then we'll think this through and regroup."

Char grabbed a brightly colored stoneware plate and deposited romaine onto it with silver tongs.

As she ate, Savvy looked thoughtful. "I don't get it. I mean, I get Ryder using his star power, but why cover up in a uniform? He'd be much more recognizable without that phony getup. Unless—do you think he's actually a real firefighter?"

"The reporter asked that question, but I was already on my way back to the car. I wanted to stop and hear his answer, but I didn't want to let on how interested I was."

Savvy wiped her mouth with a linen napkin, smoothed it on the marble counter, and reflected.

"If he's a real fireman, that *is* pretty formidable. Maybe the department just let him wear the uniform as a costume. After all, Ryder's helping their cause. Still, I know something you have that Ryder McBride doesn't."

Char raised an eyebrow in doubt. "Yeah? What?"

"Us," she said, still munching, indicating Meri and herself with a nonchalant wave of her fork.

Chapter 16

Sunday, June 22

At church the next morning, Char and her sisters witnessed a revelation.

Though they sat in their usual spot toward the left front, the rows around them were desolate. Only the few faithful who presumably hadn't seen last night's TV coverage of Ryder McBride, movie-star-slash-fireman, were in their corner.

Most everyone else was jammed into the rear of the sanctuary, toward the right.

It was amazing how quickly the tide had turned. He'd only been back in town a couple of weeks, and *wham,* everyone had Ryder fever.

Meri raised an eyebrow at Char. "Looks like we're no longer the cool kids," she whispered.

"Sometimes you get what you pray for," Char replied.

For years, this was what she thought she had wanted. The simple gift of sitting in public, in her hometown, and being treated like just another citizen.

And now that she'd received that gift, she had strangely mixed feelings about it.

The girls had always lived with a schizophrenic combination of attention and neglect. They were still dealing with their abandonment, in varying degrees. The day Maman had left had been the defining moment of their childhood.

When the gospel reading was finished, Char settled in for the sermon. But as hard as she tried to concentrate on Father Ed, her mind kept going back to that terrible time.

It wasn't all that bad. That was the psychological Band-Aid she used when she allowed the memories to surface. It was her best defense against the feelings of resentment and loss that accompanied the flashbacks.

Maman, sitting at her dressing table in a cloud of the bespoke rose perfume formulated for her and her alone, at a tiny boutique on the Champs-Élysées.

Maman. How many times, late at night in the grip of homesickness, had Char's dorm mates begged her to describe what it had been like growing up with a famous actress for a mother?

A mental snapshot of Savvy, tottering around on Maman's heels, while Char and Meri took turns with her silk bathrobe came to mind. They'd been pretending they were going to the awards ceremony, too . . . crowding around Maman in her white satin gown, who touched their noses with her powder puff and rouged their baby-smooth cheeks.

"Maintenant, vous êtes très jolie. There. Now, you are pretty."

Char would try to explain that Maman was the same evocative combination of warm and cool, push and pull in private that she was on-screen, but that never satisfied them. Yet that was what made Lily, *Lily*: the aloof mystique that had won her millions of fans. She was like a promise for the future that inspired hope, but never came true.

Up until the fatal crash days later, the girls hadn't even been aware that she'd run away.

At first, all they heard was a low rumbling among the staff.

"Madame est parti avec l'Argentin," whispered Jeanne, the cook.

"It was the Argentine who took her," the head housekeeper was overheard telling the au pair who had introduced them to this church where Char now sat—who'd in turn broken the bad news to the girls.

Because Papa was off who-knew-where.

Years later, from the safe distance of her school, Char pulled up the newspaper accounts on the Internet. She read that Xavier St. Pierre was initially "overcome with grief." Apparently, too overcome even to tell his daughters that Maman was dead.

How could he? she'd rationalized. The French didn't subscribe to warm, fuzzy American ideas of child rearing. He'd never established a rapport with them to begin with. How could he be expected to start then—explaining the adultery and death of his beloved Lily—when he was in the throes of his own intense suffering?

She knew it was ridiculous—the excuses left over from childhood that she still used to justify her parents' behavior. They were the excuses of a little girl struggling to make sense of her world. Still, she couldn't let go of them.

While researching her father, Char also had found out that Lily d'Amboise had been a well-known French actress way before she'd gone to Hollywood. She'd been accustomed to being worshipped, catered to . . . adored. Within four short years, she migrated to a strange country, married, and produced three daughters in quick succession.

Maman must have missed acting and all that went with it, because she wasted no time going right back to it. Never really even took a break except during the later parts of her pregnancies.

People took care of *Lily*, not the other way around. Who could fault poor Maman for her lack of mothering skills?

And while being thrust onto a plane with one suitcase apiece was initially terrifying, with hindsight it was probably a good thing Char and her sisters had been sent east. Papa wasn't emotionally equipped to take care of them. And who knew how they'd have coped if they'd had to deal with the abrupt swing of the valley's spotlight from their mother onto them—mere kids, still in mourning?

As it was, they'd been immersed into highly structured—if separate—environments, far from the prying eyes of Hollywood and the wine coast. With hindsight, anonymity and some excellent guidance counselors had probably been their salvation.

Not that it had been easy—far from it. Char recalled the "pleasures" of Hollyhurst Academy: tiny rooms; living by the bells, from the seven o'clock wake up to lights out; communal bathrooms. And above all, the loneliness of having to grow up without her sisters.

But now they were together again. The chance to reunite was what had pulled the three back to the Napa mansion, to try to reclaim some semblance of family from whatever shreds were left.

Char blinked and tossed her head. She'd just spent the entire Nicene Creed and the Lord's Prayer reminiscing. Now Father Ed was calling them up to communion.

When she returned from the altar, she watched intently as the rear rows trickled forward, waiting with everyone else to stare at Napa's newest phenom.

A core group surrounded him. An ordinary-looking middle-aged woman in a nondescript dress led, followed by a pixie-faced brown-haired girl—twelve, if her guess was right. Ryder must've looked just like that, once upon a time. And a pair of gangly teenage boys, obviously twins . . . tall, like Ryder, but still adjusting to their height.

Ryder guided his little sister toward the priest, his hands resting lightly but protectively on her shoulders.

Probably headed home to their one-story ranch to sit down to Sunday dinner, Char imagined. With a stab of envy, she could almost smell the aroma of roasting chicken greeting them as they walked in the front door. Add a father figure, and it was the kind of family she had always dreamed of.

When it was Ryder's turn, he crossed himself and sipped from the chalice. It was a cinch to read the thoughts of those communing after him. While they were still in the church parking lot, they'd be online, bragging about drinking from the same cup as Ryder McBride. It might even be enough to bring them back again next Sunday. That made her happy for Father Ed. God knew, he needed the numbers.

On his way back to his seat, Ryder sought her eyes. Letting down her guard, she gave him an empathetic smile.

So often, people lost sight of the humanity of celebrities. They became these icons of perfection that were either envied or vilified out of all proportion.

Like Maman.

Chapter 17

A half dozen of Ryder's male teammates were pretending to retie their running shoes, while others made a show of stretching hamstrings. Their matching red Challenge tees made them stand out against the Pacific blue sky.

Across the street, a bevy of toned women warmed up, too, the white jersey of their tees stretched over curves the men didn't have. The interested glances flying back and forth energized the dry valley air.

"You think I don't know what you show-offs are doing, flexing your biceps like that?" Ryder kidded good-naturedly.

"Let them go first," laughed one of the younger men.

"Forget it," Ryder said with a knowing smile. "The only view we're gonna be seeing is the Mayacamas. The race is Friday. Each of us can do our own fartleks once we're warm. Run out to Mission Trail and back."

Then his peripheral vision caught Chardonnay St. Pierre approaching in a pair of shorts made from so little cloth they made his skivvies look like a stage curtain. From the looks of those quads, she wasn't anywhere near as delicate as she'd appeared the night they'd met, when she'd been swathed in enough white silk to make a parachute.

While his men ogled, he sauntered toward her.

"Another coincidence?" she called.

Hellcat. She drew a grin from him, in spite of himself.

Something about her always put him on the alert. He searched her expression as the distance between them closed. The woman's moods swung back and forth like a pendulum. What was he in for today?

Her smile teased, but her eyes sparkled.

He spread his arms in a fake protestation of guilt. "You caught me."

They came together on common ground in the middle of the road. She cocked a hip, hands propped on a narrow waist. Two coaches in full view of their teams, but out of their hearing.

"You may find this hard to believe, but I don't have spies watching to see when you're going to run. I take my guys out four times a week, and this is only the first time we've run into Team Chardonnay."

"Second," Char corrected him, raising two fingers.

"I was by myself that day, remember?"

Like the wind off the bay, her face and tone shifted without warning.

"Your kid sister looks just like you."

Ryder drew a blank.

"Church last Sunday?" She gave him a slanted look.

He looked down and scuffed the toe of one sneaker on the blacktop.

"The day after Calistoga. I got a little taste of how it feels to be you up there," he said.

"How'd you like it?" she replied, her mocking tone gone. "Sometimes I feel like I'm on stage myself."

He shrugged and smiled. "That's showbiz."

"What about your family?"

Ryder's smile faded. "I can take care of them all right."

"I never said you couldn't. What about your dad? Does he ever go to church with you?"

He'd seen her sarcastic side, but he hadn't taken her for a mean girl. He searched her face for an overlooked cruel streak, but found none.

She shrugged. "I'm not judging. Papa doesn't go, either."

His team was getting restless, a few running in place. He shifted his view sideways to the sun, just above the Mayacamas.

"We're burning daylight."

Char followed his eyes to the horizon.

Then she turned and peeled off toward her own group.

"Later," she called with a casual little wave.

Still sorting out what had just transpired, Ryder joined his team in watching the rhythm of her bodacious glutes contract and relax as she jogged back to her friends.

No way she could have known his dad was dead. It was always in the forefront of his consciousness, but he could hardly blame her for her ignorance. After all, Ryder's family members were nobodies. His own flame was just catching spark, whereas she'd been living in a fishbowl for years, according to those who paid attention to those things—his mom, for instance. Char had apparently always been a big deal in this town, and yet Ryder had never even noticed, much less been aware that her mother was the dead actress Lily d'Amboise.

Gesturing to his team to follow, Ryder set out to the Mission Trail endpoint.

A half mile in, Dan, a crusty career man who had worked with Ryder's dad, edged up alongside him. Ryder'd known him for years, though the bit of a chip on Dan's shoulder had prevented them from growing close. But Ryder had to admit, he had an awesome cadence for a runner of his age.

"You know who she is, don't you?"

Apparently everyone did. "One of St. Pierre's girls."

"Ever met her old man?"

"Grower." Ryder panted. "Vintner. Owner of the St. Pierre label."

Ryder glanced Dan's way. And was taken aback by his dark expression.

"Owns a lot of stuff in this valley."

What was Dan getting at?

"Word is, he owns the mayor, the police chief, and half the city council."

Ryder couldn't restrain a dry laugh. Was this some kind of veiled scolding? Had Dan read about him kissing Chardonnay two Fridays ago at her father's party and disapproved? If that were the case, why didn't he just come out and say so?

"Rumors like that dog the big wheels in every town. I'd be more surprised if he *hadn't* made any allies along the way." It didn't take a degree in sociology to know that. Anyone who kept up with the news could cite a dozen ways in which politics were dictated by human nature, for better or worse.

"Just saying. The St. Pierres have always been known as ruthless cons. Since the day Yves St. Pierre sailed over from Bordeaux with his family's old rootstock, just about the time Prohibition went into effect. Piss-poor timing there. Lots of growers either left, or ripped out their grapes and planted peaches. Yves gambled it wouldn't last and went on as planned, though, making cab. Got through the dry times selling plonk to the Catholics and the Jews—made a lot of priests and rabbis rich, too, funneling a tad more'n just communion wine down to their congregations—and cellared the rest."

Dan paused in his story to let his breathing catch up with his stride.

"When Prohibition was repealed, ol' Yves was ready to rock and roll."

Ryder eyed Dan with bewilderment. "How'd you know so much about the wine business?"

"Brother-in-law's got a little operation down in Santa Rosa." Dan grinned sheepishly. "You know what they say: 'Any jackass can make wine.' It's the marketing that takes brains."

Ryder shook his head. "So both generations of the St. Pierres are shrewd businessmen. What's that have to do with Char? Besides, it was her father who invited me to their house in the first place. *He* wanted to meet *me*."

"All I'm sayin' is, watch your back. She's a St. Pierre. You can't trust her."

A rising wail from the direction of the valley floor snapped Ryder's head back to the present.

Like a school of red fish, Ryder and his team of firefighters executed a smooth one-eighty in perfect unison, turning back in the direction of their cars. What had been a controlled, moderate pace accelerated to a group sprint.

Chapter 18

Meri's hand flew to her mouth. Her tablet sat propped in front of her on the breakfast table, among small crystal bowls of oranges and honeydew sliced earlier by Jeanne, the cook.

"Here you two are again, on NapaUnbound!"

Savvy and Char eyed each other over their porcelain teacups. Meri had always had a gift for melodrama, no doubt inherited from Maman.

"Let me see," said Char, putting down her éclair and licking her fingertips.

Meri looked up round-eyed.

Char took a steadying breath and reached for the tablet.

Meri was right. This shot showed them standing in the middle of Solano Avenue, the Mayacamas serving as a conveniently picturesque backdrop.

The photo was taken during their brief conversation before yesterday's run.

"At least you're not *indelicato* in this one." Meri giggled.

Char frowned.

"Sucking face," Savvy chipped in.

"Funny." Char flashed a sarcastic grin.

"Now this had to be one of his runners with a phone camera. There were no paps around. I was on my guard the whole time."

"They got you in your running shorts," said Savvy.

"More like bikini bottoms!" added Meri, scowling and looking over Char's shoulder. "What the heck, Char?!"

"Oh, Meri. When did you become such a prude? They're called briefs, and everyone's wearing them."

"Hold on! Scroll down there." Meri pointed to the bottom of the page.

"More stuff."

Char's heart leaped when she saw the full-page close-up of Ryder. His cool LA haircut was matted with sweat, one anvil-shaped cheekbone was stained with soot, and his stubbled jawline was gritted. It was a candid shot of a rugged workingman caught up in the midst of a dangerous job, oblivious to the camera. He just happened to be drop-dead gorgeous. And, oh yeah, Hollywood royalty.

Pulse pounding, her eyes flew to the text accompanying the photograph.

It's Not an Act—Ryder McBride's the Real Deal Firefighter Follows in Father's Footsteps

"What's that mean—his 'father's footsteps'?"

Sharp-eyed fans of Napa native Ryder McBride spotted the actor disguised in a bright yellow slicker and helmet last Saturday in Calistoga. McBride was acting as spokesman for a team passing the boot for the Firefighters' Relief Fund, a nonprofit that provides assistance to the victims of fires.

While his role as filmdom's leading man is unassailable, Saturday's sighting led some to question whether McBride has the right to wear the uniform of a real "first responder," other than on a movie set.

But Wednesday's brushfire off Western Avenue was

no publicity stunt. McBride again appeared decked out in Napa city gear to help extinguish the blaze.

Char inhaled sharply, looked up at Meri, and pointed to the text.

"Yesterday while my team was running along Solano, we heard sirens and saw Ryder and his team hightailing it back to their cars."

McBride has a history of civic service. Records in San Jose reveal he was a reservist while a student at SJ State. NapaUnbound has learned that this summer, he's signed on with the Napa city station, between learning his lines and bulking up for his latest film, Triple Play.

She turned to Savvy. "This says he actually volunteers for Napa city."

"Well, whaddaya know. He's legit," said Savvy.

Ryder's late father, Roland McBride, was a career fire-fighter who lost his life battling the Southside Migrant Farmworker Camp inferno seven years ago, leaving behind a wife and four children, of whom Ryder is the eldest.

While he couldn't be reached for comment, that tragic incident from his past might well explain McBride's involvement in the FRF.

Char stopped reading and closed her eyes to steady herself. "What is it?" asked Savvy, an edge to her voice.

Silently, Char read on.

For the first time, the FRF is vying against some of the valley's most well-established charities for a grand prize of one million dollars in the Napa Charity Challenge, the McDaniel Foundation's premier charitable event. Sources estimate that the FRF collected over ten thousand dollars in cash and pledges over the first weekend, thanks in large part to McBride's appeal.

Notably, the only other new organization competing in the challenge is Chardonnay's Children, founded by the Domaine St. Pierre heiress. Xavier St. Pierre was the owner of the camp where Roland McBride was killed in the line of duty.

The story was accompanied by page after page of old photos from both the McBride and St. Pierre families, and an aerial of the Southside Migrant Camp.

The blood drained from Char's face.

Seeing her pale, Savvy pulled up the story on her own device.

The room was still while she brought herself up to speed.

"Okay." Savvy leaped up in her take-charge way, spreading her fingers in a gesture of calm. "Let's all take a deep breath here, shall we? First of all, there's no hard evidence that this story is true. And even if it is, no one's blaming Papa for Roland McBride's death. Even if he really was an owner at the time—and we don't know that he was—there were no charges filed in the case of that migrant camp fire. If there had been, we surely would've known that. And Papa's insurance no doubt took care of the victims' families. So let's not get our panties in a twist.

"And secondly, these are archive photos. I've seen them before, in old newspapers. It's not like someone broke into our house and got previously unpublished pictures."

Stiffly, Char stood too, and strode barefoot across the cold terracotta tiles, thinking on her feet. "Yesterday when Ryder and I were running, I asked him whether or not his dad went to church."

She spun back around to face them. "How was I supposed to know the poor man was—" She choked on the word, unable to finish. "And now, I find out our family was involved in his death. . . ."

"Char. Don't," said Savvy.

"Accident or not, we're *involved*," Char added, a deep frown creasing her forehead.

She pressed her temples and paced back the other way.

"He'll never speak to me again. Why should he?"

Meri flashed Savvy a look that pleaded for her to say something smart. Then she went to Char and tossed an arm around her shoulders.

"Would everybody just chill?" asked Savvy. "You're jumping to conclusions, Char. Even if Papa was involved—tangentially, of course—you've done nothing wrong. There's no guilt by association."

Char gave her an incredulous look.

"What are you talking about? Of course there's guilt by association! Guilt and humiliation. All of our lives, every stupid thing this family's done has reflected on us. That's how it's always been. It's what drives us! It's why Meri was so anxious to make a name in the art world that she quit school early, the minute she got a little recognition! It's why you were obsessed with scoring a four-point-oh all the way through college and getting into a top law school!"

It was also behind Char's deep-seated need to give back to others from the great, unearned wealth that had come to them merely by virtue of being born St. Pierres.

But shame was only part of what motivated them. It was also about unique self-worth. *Real* worth, not the number that was their bank account. And now, here was yet another disgraceful scandal for them to live down.

It had happened seven years ago. But thanks to Ryder's newfound fame and some Jack Russell journalism, within a matter of hours everyone in the valley would be talking about how Xavier St. Pierre had made an orphan out of their favorite son.

Tension blanketed the room while the sisters looked at the floor . . . the table . . . out the window at the sunshine reflecting off the palm-tree–lined pool. Anywhere to avoid seeing the pain in each other's eyes.

Meri set down the tablet. "Stop torturing yourself over the past," she choked, enfolding Char in her arms.

Char sniffed and stepped out of her embrace.

"Meri! Don't you see? Tomorrow night I have to face him at Diablo."

"No, you don't," said Meri, blinking back tears. "You can quit. You aren't obligated to do any of this."

"I'm not a quitter. But it's not just the race. Do you realize the implications that article will have?"

"Meri's right. There's no reason to put yourself through this." Savvy stepped forward authoritatively, hands on her hips. "Char, you've always pushed yourself so hard. The volunteering. The field hockey. The running." Her sternness softened to maternal concern. "When will you learn that you can't outrun our past?"

"NapaUnbound said Ryder's face has already helped him raise five figures in one day!" Char went on, ignoring Savvy's question. "And when word gets out that he's a for-real fireman—and his dad died in the line of duty . . . *and it was Papa's fault* . . . Ryder's donations are going to go through the roof, and mine are going to dry up like an arroyo in August."

"What is this arroyo?"

All three women jumped when Papa entered the kitchen in an artfully rumpled plaid button-down.

He kissed their cheeks in the European manner, enveloping Char in his aura of tobacco and patchouli. Then he fixed himself a shot of espresso from the state-of-the-art machine tucked away on the counter.

Char had friends who swooned over Papa's old-world manners. But sometimes, instead of the air-kisses, all she wanted was a big old American bear hug.

"*Ça va, Papa?*" asked Savvy, covering up with a forced smile.

"*Ça va bien,*" he replied in his familiar gravely tone. "Tomorrow is Friday. Are you prepared for the party?"

Only Meri and Savvy nodded their assent.

Char turned away to swipe a tear away before her father noticed, but she needn't have worried. As usual, he was too caught up in his own thoughts and plans to notice his daughters' agitation.

Char couldn't help but compare Papa to the suave, silver-haired "world's most interesting man" in the old beer commercial. Like him, Papa was usually surrounded by gorgeous women. She waited to see what glamorous stranger might be tagging along after him this morning, but he was alone—for the time being.

He picked up the mail from where the housekeeper had laid it and thumbed through the periodical on the top of the pile.

"*Regardez.* Chardonnay, your name is here, in *Napa Lifestyles.*"

Three pairs of female eyes met in apprehension.

"I had completely forgotten the McDaniel Foundation race was this Saturday."

Papa hadn't seemed surprised, back when Char had told him about her charity. He'd indulged her philanthropic whims for years, just as she knew the others in the valley humored her back when she was a teenager. But they'd never had an in-depth conversation about Chardonnay's Children. Despite her new degree, Papa had no clue how deeply committed she was to public service.

Papa sat down, folded back the page, and kept reading.

"Fruit?" asked Meri, spooning some pale green melon chunks into a bowl.

Without looking up, he grunted his thanks when she handed him the dish. Then a scowl formed above his eyebrows. Red crept up his neck inch by inch, until it flooded his cheeks.

"Salaud! What swine wrote this?" he spat, scanning the page for the author's byline.

The girls hadn't read the *Napa Lifestyles* version of the Ryder story, but it was easy to guess what was in it.

"Is it true, Papa?" asked Char quietly.

Papa jumped to his feet, tossing the magazine across the counter.

"If you are asking me if I owned the Southside Migrant Camp, the answer is yes. But this reporter, he did not"—he looked up, pinching together his thumb and two fingers as he searched for the phrase— "do his due diligence."

With baited breath, the girls waited for him to go on.

"Yes, it is true, I—along with some partners—did own this migrant camp, but I did not manage it. It was run by what is called an ag management company. I paid them a very large sum of money to oversee it."

The sisters exhaled as one.

Char stepped forward. "What caused the fire?" she asked softly. Prying risked Papa's further wrath, but she had to know.

"What is the difference what caused the fire? Do you think it was I who caused it? Of course not! This fire, it was an accident! The insurance company and the fire marshal, they all say I am innocent!"

He tossed back his espresso.

"For what reason is this written about now, after seven long years?!"

Char stared at her half-eaten chocolate éclair, her appetite gone.

Could she take Papa at his word or was he covering for yet another one of his major faux pas?

Even if Papa was telling the truth and the fire had truly been an accident, one thing was still for sure. Ryder McBride would never forgive her or her family for their role—no matter how minor—in his dad's death.

Char dreaded bringing it up, but Papa was already agitated, so bracing herself, she rushed the words out before she lost her nerve.

"Papa, I'm going to have to miss the party tomorrow night. There's a pasta dinner at Diablo for the kickoff of the race the next morning. All of the team leaders are expected to be there."

None of his daughters had ever missed a Friday night fete. Papa affected a shocked expression.

"What is this?" he bellowed. "You are going to disappoint your papa?" His chin lifted in defiance. *"Non, mademoiselle.* At this, I put down my toe."

He raised a finger in emphasis. "You will have the pasta here, at our home, on Friday. You will not be missed at Diablo. It is the race that is important, not the eve of the race."

Char swallowed his graceless insult, fighting to keep her voice calm.

"The kickoff dinner is very important, Papa. We train as a team, we carbo-load as a team, and we run as a team. I wouldn't be much of a leader if I skipped it."

Just then a slim, bed-headed stranger entered the kitchen. A shirt Char recognized as Papa's covered her down to mid-thigh, from where a tattoo snaked all the way down to her ankle.

"I heard yelling," the woman said.

Exasperated, Papa's head swiveled between the four women in his kitchen.

"D'accord—bien!" he roared, gesturing broadly. "Go! Go to your dinner of second-rate pasta while your papa serves the finest beef-steak and seafood and wines in America, to the most prominent guests to be found anywhere in the world!"

From the entrance to the room, the doe-eyed stranger lifted a brow.

Papa turned on his heel and gave his elbow to his lady friend, only to abruptly spin back around. After reaching into his pocket, he peeled some bills from a bulky money clip and slapped them onto the counter.

"Here!" He directed to Char. "You will take this for your *leettle* race!" He stared down his aquiline nose, huffed in triumph, and walked away with the woman on his arm. She turned, gave the girls an apologetic smile and the merest shrug, and they turned the corner. Back to bed.

Meri and Savvy barely held back until they were sure he was gone before collapsing in a gale of muffled snickers. "Who *was* that?" asked Meri rhetorically.

"The girl with the snake tattoo," snorted Savvy, and they howled again. Xavier's daughters were way past getting bent out of shape over his lovers. It was easier to laugh at them than cry.

But Char didn't join in the laughter; she only sighed with relief. She'd been agonizing for days about how she was going to break the news to Papa about the pasta dinner. Now, at least that was over.

Still chuckling, Meri scampered over and gleefully scooped up the money. "Let's see how much," she crowed. Papa had his faults, but he could afford to cater to his daughters when it suited him.

The three had the nonchalant attitude toward money only possessed by the very wealthy. A thick wad of bills lying on the kitchen counter wouldn't ordinarily have evoked any reaction whatsoever. But this money was different because it was earmarked for Char's cause.

As she riffled through the twenties, Meri's eyes grew.

"Don't bother," said Char, taking the bills and smacking them back on the counter. "I'm not taking that money. I made a decision at the very outset of this competition that I don't want Papa's help. This is something I have to do on my own."

Savvy spoke first.

"Char, we get that you want to do this without Papa. But don't go overboard. There's not a competitor out there who'd turn down that chunk of change. You want to win this thing, don't you? Think of the children."

"I never *stop* thinking about those children."

"Then why reject Papa's offer of help? Don't you want to win the million? For the kids?"

"Of course I want to win—but by doing it my own way. Don't you see? If I take Papa's money, I'll be setting a precedent. Everyone will know I took the easy way out."

"How?" asked Meri. "How will anyone know who gave what?"

"Transparency," explained Savvy. "The law requires charities to make their list of donors available for public scrutiny."

"Exactly. If it became known that Papa was underwriting my operation, why would anyone else be motivated to help? I want this foundation to take wing, to grow. If I start accepting Papa's donations now, where would it end? Chardonnay's Children might as well be called Xavier's Children. And with Papa's reputation, that could mean it's over before it even begins."

Her sisters winced.

Char placed a hand on each of their arms.

"It's not you two I want to distance myself from; you know that. It's the old St. Pierre reputation. The scandals, the arrests, the drugs . . . all of it. That's not me; it's not you, either. It's the fallout we've inherited. I want to change all that. Create a new St. Pierre image. Admit it. You'd like that, too."

"It's way too late to change the way people think about Xavier St. Pierre," Savvy said, her mouth thin with distaste.

"I know." Char sighed, She popped the rest of her éclair into her mouth purely out of need for chocolate rather than her nonexistent appetite and licked her fingers. "But maybe I can be the one to start a chain of events that transforms the way they think about *us*. Wouldn't it be an amazing by-product of my foundation if the next generation of St. Pierres were talked about primarily for their good works, instead of their transgressions?"

Chapter 19

Friday, June 27

Ryder bent his tall frame over the low sink and splashed cold water on his face. It wasn't until he'd gotten a fancy apartment in LA that he'd recognized how dated the bathroom was in this old house. As soon as his *First Responder* checks started rolling in, he'd help his mom remodel it any way she chose.

He squinted into the mirror at his bloodshot eyes. Bed was calling him back, but he'd been thrashing in the sheets for hours unable to sleep, waiting for dawn to break.

Down the hall, the coffeepot clinked against his mother's mug, signaling that she was up. Finally he could ask her the questions that had been swirling through his head all night long.

He padded out to the kitchen to find her pulling orange juice from the fridge.

"Good morning. Can I pour you some?" she said, the carton poised.

"Yeah." The word came out as a croak, the mere effort sending him into a coughing spasm.

"Whew. You look kind of rough. How's your throat?"

Both knew what inhaling brush smoke could do to a man's lungs. "Fine." He hacked again and took a swig of juice. "Agh!" The juice burned like acid going down, prompting more maternal doting. "Maybe skip the juice today." She got a new glass and ran the tap. "Drink some water. If that doesn't clear up by tomorrow, I want you to go see Dr. Cortez."

"It's got to—*cough*—clear up. I got a race to run."

"Oh, Ryder! The half-marathon! Here, try something warm," she said, pouring him a coffee.

"Are you hungry? It's only seven. Bridget and the boys won't be up for another hour, but I can make . . ."

Ryder shook his head, went to the window, and peered out between the white ruffled curtains.

Then he turned back to face her, leaning against the Formica counter.

"I won't be home for supper tonight. There's a kickoff dinner for the race, up at Diablo."

"I see. Will Chardonnay be there?"

"Everyone will be there."

He couldn't wait to lay eyes on her again. Her killer body, her hypnotic blue eyes. And she actually had some deep thoughts under all that silky blond hair. The woman was the whole package.

But his mom was giving him one of her worried looks again.

"Mom. What?" He spread his arms and raised his brow. "What is it that everyone has against me and Char?"

"What do you mean? Who else said something?"

"Dan. Yesterday he was filling my head with all sorts of rumors about the St. Pierres. Warned me not to trust them."

She hesitated, then spoke, choosing her words carefully.

"It's not that I dislike Char, dear. Far from it. I just don't like that your agent used her for a publicity stunt."

"Mom, I told you. Amy does what she's paid to do—what everybody does. There's nothing inherently wrong with publicity."

"There's nothing wrong until somebody gets hurt. But unfortunately, in this case she's making money by exposing people's misfortune. Digging up their private lives . . . their mistakes, and their family's mistakes."

Ryder set his empty glass in the sink. "What mistakes? What's so awful about a photograph of a single man giving a single woman a kiss good night?"

"Because it wasn't her choice, that's why. You ambushed her."

He threw up his hands in concession. "I know. You're right, Mom. But we talked about it, and we're past it now."

Thoughtfully, she looked down at the table, then changed tack and rose.

"Well, I'm glad to hear it. Let me get you some breakfast . . ."

Ryder shoved off from the counter, the sudden movement igniting a fresh hacking spell.

"Not hungry yet." He cleared his throat. "Maybe when the others get up. Think I'll go study my lines for an hour."

He wouldn't be able to concentrate on his script this morning, but he wanted to be alone to revel in his anticipation over seeing Char tonight.

Chapter 20

Char drove up to Diablo alone.

As supportive as they were, Meri and Savvy didn't relish consuming all those starchy calories alongside Char's exuberant team of field hockey players.

Not that her sisters weren't helping. Meri was designing an original silver necklace for the auction, and Savvy was donating a free legal consultation, plus manning the donation website. And both were actively scouring the valley for more contributions in their free time.

Besides, Papa would really have kittens if all three of them missed his dinner party.

Although now Char was beginning to wish she were staying home, too.

She drove northward in the fading summer light, knowing that the news about the Southside Migrant Camp fire would be fresh in everyone's mind, thanks to that story in the press. The nearer she got to Diablo, the more she dreaded walking into the restaurant. Would she enter to find people whispering behind their hands? Might some actually hold her culpable for a tragedy that happened seven years ago, when she wasn't even in California?

She told herself she was blowing things out of proportion, but experience had taught her just the opposite. Napa Valley had an air of sophistication, but the native population was small and news traveled fast. And the irony of this story was just too juicy to ignore.

Two ambitious young upstarts, pitted against each other by circumstances: female against male ... one richly bred and poorly raised, the other the son of a simple public servant ... whose families were intertwined with disaster.

With a scoop like that, the other teams would be lucky to get any press at all.

Yet what worried Char most was Ryder's reaction. How would he be taking the news? Would he treat her any differently? Blame her for his dad's death? What if he completely shunned her? That dreadful possibility sunk in her belly like a twenty-pound dumbbell.

Because for some reason, she liked Ryder. Yeah, he was gorgeous. That was a given. But there was more to this movie star than that. He had substance. Intelligence. A curious mind that she found infinitely more alluring than mere good looks.

And the way he'd commanded her eyes when he kissed her ... how his hand seared her skin through her thin silk top the other night ...

But now everything had changed. And she was terrified of how he would react and how he might treat her.

She made an admittedly cowardly decision. As much as she wanted to be near him, she would stay out of his way tonight. He'd no doubt be relieved not to be forced to converse with the daughter of the man who was implicated in his father's death.

But then she remembered: He didn't read the stuff that was written about himself. Or so he said. She could only hope.

Ryder maneuvered a seat to face the door. When Char entered Diablo, a jolt of electricity crackled across the room, connecting them, and he started to rise from his seat. But when their eyes met, hers seemed guarded, worried. And then she looked away.

His heart sank and then so did his butt. Instead of the warmth he'd been hoping for, now this.

Christ, the woman's moods were as unpredictable as a house fire in a windstorm. Pride shaken, he nodded a curt greeting and then went back to his plate. But his appetite for his fettuccine was gone.

Is this how she wanted to play it? Warm one day, cool the next? So be it. He'd use tonight for what it was meant to be: team building, pure and simple.

Life had been way simpler before he'd started dealing with her, anyway, and now was an excellent time to stop. Right now, on the eve of the half. He'd run better, anyway, without the distraction of a woman on his mind. Even if she was hot and smart and interesting all at the same time.

No, there was nothing forcing Ryder to interact with Char, simply because they'd be in the same room tonight, loading up on carbs. He would just hang with his team and pay no mind to the woman who'd been mucking up his life from the moment he'd run into her.

But even looking down at his plate, an intense awareness of her body as she threaded her way through the tables lingered. And all through the meal and the rallying speeches, he couldn't shake the impression that she felt his presence, too.

A wave of white foam sloshed over the side of the third pitcher of beer when the waitress thumped it down. Ryder's mates refilled their mugs, their voices growing louder in the rising din of the rustic eatery.

The long, narrow room was coming alive with talk, music, and movement, now that the plates were being cleared. The athletes hopped between tables, touching base with friends from competing teams, trying to assuage the prerace jitters.

Ryder turned down a fourth pitcher and asked for the check.

High time he rounded up his team. He shook his head when he spotted several of his men up at the bar. He liked the occasional beer as much as the next guy, but he was dead serious about winning this race. He wanted that building.

As he sidestepped his way to the front, he glimpsed another familiar face there, her pretty pink lips sipping from a water glass with a lemon slice wedged on its rim.

For the last two hours they'd avoided each other, but there was no going back now. Much as he hated to be a buzzkill, he wanted to get his men out of there, and he had to pass by her to do it.

He reached the bar just in time to overhear Dan complaining bitterly to Joe, the FRF treasurer.

"If you ask me, the St. Pierres have a hell of a long way to go to make up for what they've taken away from this valley."

A sturdy woman in a tee with the Chardonnay's Children logo on the back jabbed Dan on the shoulder. At just under six feet tall, she stood eye to eye with Dan.

"Just a minute, mister. For your information, Chardonnay St. Pierre has already done 'a hell of a lot' for this valley. She's worked at the food bank, raised money for a bunch of charities, and advocated for migrants. So I don't think—"

"Lady, I don't give two shits what you think." Dan eyed her critically. "If Princess St. Pierre really wants to atone for her old man's sins, she oughta be running this race for the firemen, not the Mexicans. St. Pierre thinks the Southside catastrophe's all water under the bridge. That a firefighter's life was expendable—"

Smack!

The woman's palm made solid contact with Dan's face.

Suddenly Ryder remembered where he'd seen her before: running with Char's team out along Solano.

Dan blinked in stunned confusion. His fingertips flew to his jaw, his green eyes growing mean. Then, faster than a shot, he jabbed his aggressor in the center of her breastbone with the heel of his hand.

She staggered. Flushing, she regained her footing. Among the crowd, the risk-averse edged away, while the curious swelled forward.

"Stop it!" Char somehow reached in, a willow between two oaks, and planted a palm on each combatant's chest. *What the hell was she doing?* Neither one paid the slightest attention to her, let alone budged.

But then the amazon lunged again, inciting a wicked grin to overspread Dan's face. She might be big, but he was experienced. He blocked with his left arm while his right grabbed a fistful of her shirt. He yanked forward and then shoved back, slamming her butt-first into two other women, toppling all three in a domino effect.

It was enough to have given most people whiplash. But this one still wasn't through. She was up in a flash, yanking off a bystander's restraining hand.

Someone screamed, and the bartender grabbed his phone.

Ryder had never pegged Dan for the type who'd lay hands on a woman—even if the woman *was* the size of a UCLA linebacker. The woman was a glutton for punishment. She was coming back yet again for more.

It was Hail Mary time. Ryder drew back his fist and let it fly. His knuckles scraped soft flesh en route to Dan's bony nose.

Like spin art, a fine red spray from Dan's nostrils dotted everything and everyone within range as Dan careened sideways, crashing into some chairs. There his own teammates pounced on him, grunts and yells drifting up from the floor as he tried to fight them off.

Char looked down at her white tee and gasped at the scarlet dots sprinkling it.

"We got 'em," yelled Joe from amid the bodies on the floor.

Ryder's knuckles stung like a son of a bitch. And his throat was still raw from the brushfire. But all he could think of was—*damn it*—why had Char gone and stuck her head right into the path of his fist?

He seized her by the shoulders and frantically scrutinized her face. Her cheek was beginning to pinken where he'd sideswiped her, and he reached out tentatively.

"You okay, baby?" he asked, low enough so that only she could hear.

She gave him a dazed-looking nod.

"Ice," he yelled to the bartender, his voice cracking. He caught the plastic bag midair even as he ducked his head to cough again.

"C'mon."

The cops would be there any minute. He snatched one of Char's hands, pressed the crunchy cold icepack into her other one, then used his body to carve a path toward the door, dragging her behind.

To hell with the team.

And if she wanted to sue him later for socking her, she could. But right now all he could think of was getting her out of there, out of the public eye.

As Ryder hauled her through the parking lot toward his pickup, the wail of a distant siren grew louder by the second.

He swung open the passenger door, stuffed her in, and sprinted around to the driver's side.

"What about my car?"

"Throw me your keys. I'll drive you up to get it tomorrow, after the race. Or, if you're tied up, I've got two kid brothers who'd love to get their hands on a CL-Class."

"This is all my fault," she said as the truck lurched over the curb and turned south on 29. "I was avoiding you tonight, but that was wrong. We need to talk. . . ."

A sickening shame washed over her as she faced the inevitability of discussing Papa's connection to the migrant camp fire.

But Ryder's thoughts were clearly elsewhere.

"Just keep that ice on your face while I get us out of here."

Gingerly, she touched the coolness to her cheekbone. She couldn't decide which hurt most: the bruise, the ice, or the fact that gossip about Papa had ruined the prerace supper for everyone.

A single black-and-white car, lights flashing, passed them going in the opposite direction.

"Thanks," she said in a subdued voice.

"You can't afford any more notoriety."

Char lowered the ice pack and turned to him. "How do you know?"

Here it came. She braced herself for his accusations.

When he didn't respond, she asked more sharply, "What about my notoriety?"

It was making her crazy, not knowing what he knew.

In the dark, he sighed audibly.

"My mom told me some stuff. She's lived in Napa city all her life. She knows everyone. Hears everything."

"Like what, exactly?" Char braced herself for the worst, taking scant comfort in the idea that he couldn't be that outraged, or he wouldn't be here, driving her home. Or—to wherever they were headed.

"It's not important." Whatever dreck he'd heard, he was downplaying it. That much was for sure.

"How's your cheek? Keep that ice on it."

"Just tell me what you've heard. I'll tell you which parts are true or not."

He slid down the windows, letting in the night air—unusually balmy for early June—and combed his fingers through his hair.

Char sat stiffly, waiting. But after a few minutes, the steady whoosh of tires on pavement helped normalize her heart rate, and her spine relaxed a bit. There, in the shadowy cab of his truck, his striking good looks were obscured. And he couldn't see her, either . . . or her top-of-the-line running shoes . . . her one-of-a-kind silver jewelry. For the moment, he wasn't an egotistical movie star, and she wasn't an empty-headed heiress. For just this moment, she could almost pretend they were ordinary people with ordinary lives.

And ordinary, if powerful, feelings.

She nursed a perverse hope that he might still be aware of her rose perfume, even with the cross breeze from the open windows diluting it.

"Okay. To start, Mom said you were pretty well known around here."

Char rolled her eyes and made a face, though it was useless in the gloom.

"You can do better than that. You want some help? How's this: I have four living male relatives, and all of them have been in jail at least once. Even as we speak, my cousin is locked up in the drug treatment facility in Corcoran.

"The last time Papa was arrested was just last week, for shooting at an eagle on our property—I know you heard about that," she added with a heavy dose of sarcasm. "Props to Miranda. Is that enough? Hold on, 'cause I'm just getting started. Maman left us for some lowlife player when I was ten and got herself killed in a car crash down in South America. My sisters and I were sent packing, all the way across the country. And ever since, Papa's been an active member of the tramp-of-the-month club."

That last remark made Ryder laugh, which led to a coughing spasm.

"Are you okay?"

He nodded vigorously but couldn't yet speak.

Then Char remembered.

"The fire alarm, when you tore off in the middle of your run yesterday! We saw you and your team, hightailing it back to your cars . . . and then you were on the evening news, fighting that brushfire."

He snorted. "That's the press for you—making it all about one part-time firefighter. Did the reporter even talk to the chief?"

"You didn't see the news?"

"I told you before, it's not like I google myself every morning."

He took a swig from the water bottle in the console, which calmed his windpipe.

"How are you going to run tomorrow with that sore throat?"

Dark as it was, she sensed his droll smile from the way his chin rose.

"Best you worry about yourself, little lady," he said in a bad John Wayne imitation. "Team Chardonnay's gonna get an ass-kicking tomorrow."

He was being incredibly generous, using humor to let her off the hook before she'd confessed the most damning part of her lurid family history.

"Are you talkin' trash to me?" she teased back.

"I'm dead serious. I just run for fun. But Dan runs an eight-minute mile. He's my main man."

And now, to her disappointment, they were almost at her house.

He turned right at the tasteful "Domaine St. Pierre" sign.

So. He was taking her home. This was the first time they'd ever been truly alone together, and now it was ending.

Despite the disaster at Diablo, she couldn't remember the last time she'd felt so gloriously alive.

Chapter 21

Ryder paused at a fork in the drive. Mercedes, BMWs, and Range Rovers clogged the right branch.

"Looks like Papa's party's still going full swing. Take a left."

He turned the wheel toward the business side of the winery, now deserted, his headlights picking out neatly lettered signs: Visitors' Parking, Production Facilities, Caves, and Gardens.

It was an unlikely time for a tour.

Char pointed to a large outbuilding. "You can park behind there."

He pulled up next to a tractor and cut the engine.

"Sorry, but I wasn't ready to go in the house yet."

"And . . . you also didn't want to take me in."

She paused. "Yes," she admitted. "I mean, no. I mean, I don't know."

Ryder snorted softly. "You think I have paps in there?" He had his pride, too.

She dismissed that with a disillusioned look, then turned toward the open window and inhaled deeply. "It's a beautiful night. Smell the honeysuckle? Let's get out."

An errant flame of anticipation sparked inside him. She started down a path, and he found himself trotting after her like a Pomeranian behind a Beverly Hills socialite.

"These are chardonnay vines," she said, fingering a branch. "There's no fruit on them yet, just these tiny green berries. Did you know that even white wine comes from purple grapes?"

"Not much of a drinker. Just a beer now and then."

His eyes were already adjusting to the dark. The limbs on a single peach tree were silhouetted black against a moon that was close to full.

Char reached back and took his hand. "Come on. I want to show you something."

They hiked through a neat furrow, across the field and up a rise, where she stopped and gazed back on the mansion and the ribbon of highway below.

"This is the heart of our chardonnay plantings. The very center of a tiny microclimate. The *terroir* here is different from that even one hectare away—right across the road. Those blocks are planted in merlot. Up there"—she pointed north—"is cab."

"All vineyards look the same to me, even in broad daylight."

He planted his hands on his hips and peered out on the moonlit scenery.

"Who taught you about grapes? Your dad?"

She huffed. "Hardly. Jorge, our vineyard manager, started giving me some pointers a long time ago. Before I was sent away."

"Must have been tough—being uprooted like that."

"Children don't have a choice, do they? They have to take whatever fate hands them. I suppose that's what drew me to my work with migrant kids."

He went quiet, thinking about children and fate.

And fires.

"View's impressive," he admitted.

"When my sisters and I were small, the vineyard was our playground. Neither of our parents were around much, and the au pairs they hired were barely out of their teens, so we were left to run wild, out here in the middle of nowhere. Even then, I knew it was magical. But it didn't last. There were lots of lonely nights at prep school—even college—when I worried I'd never find my way back."

"Tell me about your mom," he said.

Char gazed out at the stars. Where to start? How much to tell?

"I've been asked about her a million times. Have you seen any of her movies?"

"Who hasn't? *Fairmount Park* is a classic."

"Then you've seen her film persona. Cool—as in distant. I wish I could tell you she was warm and fuzzy off-screen. It's not that she was mean; she loved us in her own aloof way. Maman was already in her late twenties and famous before she ever came to the states, married Papa, and got pregnant. She was the only child of a much older couple—what used to be called a midlife baby. So along with that natural French reserve, she'd been pampered all her life. She never really learned how to nurture."

He felt a stab of empathy, as much for her actual history as for the pitiful excuse she'd made up to absolve her mom from being a poor parent.

"Papa always had a thing for actors. Still does."

"Is that why you don't like them?" he asked.

She looked taken aback.

"You made it pretty clear, the night we met."

She considered before replying. "There are actors, and then there are actors. Let's just say that most of the ones I've known were only looking out for themselves. What about *your* mom?" she asked.

That caught him off guard. Suddenly, he decided his mom was perfect—warts and all—compared to Char's.

"She's a good mom. No complaints. A little overprotective at times, but then she has to be. . . ."

They were headed toward dangerous territory. All well and good for him to feel sorry for someone else, but he hated being the object of pity himself. Because of that, he rarely opened up about what had happened seven years ago.

Ryder's head turned back toward the ridges, but his vision turned inward. He had just turned nineteen when it happened. Too young to have considered researching the ownership of the Southside Migrant Camp, even if he hadn't just taken on the sudden burden of becoming the man of the family. There'd been more immediate concerns than going after blame.

At Mom's insistence, he'd gone on to San Jose State, as planned. It wasn't easy, carrying a full class load and working, but he got through two and a half years. Thanks to his academic scholarship, tuition wasn't a problem, and he had tons of friends for moral support.

Then, the day before the special mass honoring the third anniversary of Dad's death, he'd come home early to find his mom still at work and the mailbox stuffed with late notices. When he laid them out before her, she broke down and admitted it. The insurance money from the fire was running out, and they were barely getting by. She hadn't wanted him to know—had wanted him to focus on his education. But things had been spiraling out of control for a long time. The house was near to foreclosure . . .

Ryder shook his head to clear his thoughts. All of that was in the past now.

Tell him. He doesn't read the headlines. Tell him now that Papa owned that camp where his dad got killed.

As Char watched Ryder, staring out over the fields and scattered lights of the Napa Valley, she knew this was the time. But she let her second chance slip away. Because at that very same moment, looking at his easy stance outlined by the moon, it hit her—what it was that had made Ryder an overnight success in show business.

It was his unself-conscious exterior, blended with a genuinely caring soul. His body was fit and relaxed, while his mind was thoughtful . . . determined . . . magnanimous, creating an intoxicating contrast. No wonder women from twelve to one hundred and twelve were so hot for him.

"All this," she murmured, eyeing him from behind, "*and* a firefighter?"

If he heard her, he didn't let on. But then, his modesty was part of his charm. It was clear he put others before himself. He'd decked his own team member tonight to defend one of Char's, and then whooshed her away from prying eyes. Helping others was his real talent.

She took a step, closing the distance between them. A twig snapped underfoot, and he swiveled around from the hip.

He pointed east, to the opposite side of the valley. "Those hills look like a pod of humpback whales, don't they?"

" 'America's Eden,' " purred Char. "Napa's nickname."

There atop the ridge, the night was warm and blue and still. But Char wasn't looking at the topography any longer.

From behind, she placed her hands on his shoulders, her stack of spaghetti-thin bracelets tinkling.

He turned fully then, and the moon illuminated his hazel eyes. A lock of brown hair curved perfectly across his forehead.

Seemingly of their own accord, her arms twined around his neck.

His hands found her waist, and she trembled. From his contrived PR kisses—*was that only two weeks ago?*—she already knew that their bodies fit together perfectly.

Tenderly, he touched her cheek again where he'd inadvertently hit it. Then he brushed his lips across it.

"Does it hurt?" he whispered.

"Not anymore."

"Doesn't look real swollen." He squinted. "If we're lucky, you won't even bruise. Did I say I was sorry?"

"Apology accepted," she breathed.

Her guilt tried to pry its relentless head between them. It was *she* who owed *him* an apology. At the very least, an explanation. But she pushed it away yet again, unwilling to spoil the moment.

Melting into his eyes, her fingers traveled up to caress his nape. She dropped her gaze to his mouth in a blatant invitation.

Ryder's thumb stroked her lower lip. He pulled her in closer until their bodies met, and he looked into her upturned face. Sliding his hand behind her jaw to support her head, he closed his eyes and kissed her in a way that wasn't meant for any camera. This was an intimate, lingering kiss that searched and probed her to her very depths. When he'd exhausted all the possibilities at one angle, his nose moved to the other side of hers, and he started all over again.

An overwhelming euphoria sluiced through Char, finally tugging her swollen lips into an uncontrollable smile. She tucked her chin and spit out a sound that was half laugh, half gasp.

"What?" he asked, his eyes now dark with ardor.

"I'm just so happy," she beamed. "Happy to be with Ryder McBride. The man, not the movie star."

He smiled too then and pressed his forehead against hers.

"Well, I'm happy to be with Char St. Pierre. The woman, not the heiress."

She glanced up, and the mood changed yet again. Their smiles faded as she slipped her hand beneath his shirt, sliding it across the warm, smooth skin of his back.

He responded in kind, and she reveled in the feel of his large hands spanning her bare torso. He brought one around, slid his fingers under her bra, and kneaded her nipple into a bud.

Char held her breath. His other hand unclasped her bra on the first try like a seasoned pro, but she was beyond caring how many starlets he'd probably bedded in the past year.

Her breasts freed, Ryder took possession of them. He left her mouth and tucked his head to wash first one nipple, then the other with a broad stroke of his tongue through the thin knit of her shirt, making them pucker even tighter. Her eyes closed, her head fell back, and a moan escaped from her throat into the summer night sky.

Char grasped the hem of her sweater and yanked it over her head.

Ryder's tongue swirled and painted her naked breasts as he molded them in his hands. He explored her shoulder blades, spine, and waist, down over the curves of her hips to her jeans. Bringing his mouth back to hers, his splayed fingertips dug into her behind, pressing her body into his. Instinctively she rocked against him, feeling the hard, male ridge along her belly, thrilling to her effect on him.

He held her close, one hand still planted on her rear, the other tangling her hair, the sound of their breath coming fast and hard.

His voice was hoarse in her ear. "I'm awake, right? This is happening."

Char stifled a giggle. *She was snogging Ryder McBride.* And he thought *he* was the lucky one?

She smiled. "It's happening."

"Say when," Ryder warned.

"What do you mean?"

"Say the word and we'll stop."

Fired up as he was, he couldn't take her here, among the vines, where there wasn't so much as a tree to lean up against or a blanket to lie on. Especially their first time. Because if there was going to be a first time, he'd make damn sure it was good enough for her to come back for seconds.

"I don't want to stop."

His mind was screaming foul, but his body was already revving in third gear.

"Are you sure?"

There was a smart tug on his zipper that sent her bracelets jingling. "I'm sure."

He coughed once, and her hand froze in place.

"You sure *you're* up to this?" she asked.

He laughed. "Oh, I'm *up*. I'm definitely up."

She laughed too and tossed her hair.

"You're so beautiful."

He twisted a fistful of blond mane, forcing her head back to better nuzzle the chord on her neck.

"So soft."

He touched his nose to the flower-scented skin on her shoulder.

"So sweet."

How long since he'd been with a woman? Insignificant faces flashed randomly through his mind. What with the new film, the FRF, family problems . . .

Whoa. He wasn't going there. Not now. Not with Chardonnay's heated, lithe body snuggling up tight against his, her fingers fumbling at his fly.

His head was spinning . . . caught up in the whirlwind of their mad, mutual attraction . . . the gardenlike setting . . . the incident at the bar.

When all was said and done, he was only a man, not some superhero like in the movies. He could only resist for so long Char's coaxing fingers, her supple mouth, her inviting glances.

His blood raced. The prospect of sex with Char was more than just hot bodies in motion. She'd already made a meaningless blur of all the ones who'd come before.

He aped her move with the zipper, and they comedically hopped out of their jeans, like marionettes in the hands of the gods.

The night air felt intoxicatingly cool on their exposed skin, in stark contrast to the searing heat where their skin touched.

With one arm securing her waist, he reached between her legs and she raised a knee to give access, wrapping her leg around his hip. When he touched her, she felt like everyman's dream.

"I want you, Char. I want you so bad."

"I want you, too. Right here. Right now."

He hitched her up until she was straddling him, then did his best to take the brunt of the fall to the earth.

Her hair fell forward, starlight outlining her slender hourglass form.

"Ready?" he murmured, his hands poised on her sides.

She gasped when he brought her down on him, and before they were through, she'd cried out to heaven and all the angels.

Hell yeah. This was Eden, all right. And she was his Eve.

Chapter 22

Reluctantly, Char descended from her natural high.

Their lovemaking seemed predestined. As if all the elements of the universe had coalesced tonight to ignite these fireworks.

But now that it was over she was left lying on her side in the finely sifted dirt, facing the troubling fact that she'd deceived this good-hearted, beautiful man, whose father's death was somehow perversely twisted up with Papa's life.

She shivered.

"You chilly?" Ryder leaped to his feet, then gave her a hand.

"That gesture's becoming familiar." She smiled as he pulled her up and into his warm arms. He ran his hands over her.

"You have goose bumps. Here, let's get you dressed." He swiped her sweater from the ground, shook it out, and pulled it over her head, smoothing out the wrinkles.

Char's heart was full to bursting. She couldn't remember ever feeling so taken care of. So genuinely cared for.

Sure, she'd been catered to her whole life—for a price. There'd never been a shortage of au pairs to dress her or cooks to feed her. It was the little things she'd missed out on, things she'd seen other kids experience that left a hollow feeling inside her. A father tousling his little girl's hair at the park. The mother of her roomie in sixth form, lovingly making her daughter's bed with her old quilt from home, before a long hug and teary kiss good-bye. Char had never had *that*.

Holding hands on the walk back to the truck, they could see down the long drive to where the mansion was still lit up like a birthday cake. Char halted, hesitant over which way to turn. "I wish I could smuggle you into the house unnoticed, but the party's not over yet. And I don't want to see photos of us showing up covered with dirt with leaves in our hair tomorrow morning."

"Why not? You look great with leaves in your hair." He grinned, carefully combing debris from out of some strands. "We can go to my house. It's not a mansion, but it's private. Well, except for my mom and my brothers and sister."

Char flashed him a tight smile. That wouldn't do, either. She started walking again toward his truck, pulling him along behind her.

"It's not that I'm trying to hide this . . . *us*," she said when they were once more sitting inside of it.

He leaned across the console to kiss her, and when she turned her head to meet his, her eye caught a glimpse of a challenge pamphlet tucked behind the seat.

"The race!" She looked around for a clock. "What time is it?"

Ryder grabbed his phone from the dash.

"Ten thirty-five." His brows knit. "I got a bunch of missed calls."

"Look." She pulled out of his arms and brushed his hair out of his eyes.

"Why don't we each sleep in our own beds tonight? We'll run the race in the morning, and then go from there."

"You won't feel like I've abandoned you?"

She melted all over again.

"You're very sweet. But I'll be fine. I'll see you again in a matter of hours."

A wave of guilt washed over her again as she hopped out at the fork in the broad driveway and watched him drive off in his old truck. Crunching down the drive, she finger-combed her hair and straightened her clothes as best she could, hoping to slip in the back door.

A matter of hours, and then she'd have to dig herself out of an even bigger mess than what she'd started with.

* * *

From the highway, Ryder returned Joe's calls. By their timing, he guessed they had to be about the bar fight.

Joe didn't pick up. No surprise, considering they had a race to run in—he glanced at the time again—eleven hours. He should've been in the sack hours ago. But if there had been a real emergency, Joe would've picked up no matter what the hour.

Back home, Ryder took a quick shower and climbed into his narrow bed, but he was too keyed up to sleep. He marveled at how fast his life had changed in one short week. This summer was to have been all about work—learning his lines, working out, helping his family and the FRF.

He often studied his script before bed as a way to commit his lines to memory, but tonight the only words he could concentrate on were those Char had breathed while he was making love to her. Visions of the vineyard ran through his head like takes from a movie, arousing him despite his need for sleep. Those lips! That body, sleek and supple as an otter! Char was as seductive as a drug. She'd left his limbs heavy with satisfaction, yet he couldn't wait to love her all over again.

He awoke to the sound of the doorbell and Joe's voice out in the kitchen.

Bolting upright, he grabbed his phone to check the time. He was due at the starting line in an hour.

Something about the sound of Joe's voice talking with his mom made Ryder uneasy. A sense of foreboding hung over him as he splashed cold water on his face, pulled on a pair of shorts, and made his way down the hall.

The second he saw Joe's face, it registered . . . a bizarre, delayed reaction to words that were only now reaching his brain. In his mind, he heard Dan's statement at Diablo all over again. And it chilled him to the bone.

"Hey, bud. Sorry to wake you . . ." Joe eyed him warily.

"What's up?"

"Dan can't run. I took him to the hospital after dinner. His nose is busted. Tried to call you last night, but I couldn't find you."

Ryder rubbed his sore knuckles. "Maybe next time he'll think twice before he shoves a woman."

His mother lowered her coffee cup. "Dan shoved a woman?" Her head swiveled from Ryder to Joe and back again. "What's going on, boys? What happened?"

Ryder opened the fridge and stared blindly into it, buying time while he figured out how to downplay last night's skirmish for Mom's sake. Couldn't Joe have just left him a voice mail or texted? Had he really had to pick this time and place to fill him in? But Mom would find out anyway. She always did.

Besides, Ryder hated secrets.

"Joe? What happened to Dan?"

Mom's relationships with the guys in the department went way back. Once a firefighter's wife, always a firefighter's wife.

"Aw, you know Dan, Mrs. McBride." Joe passed off the scuffle as negligible. "Mouth got him in trouble again. Had a few beers up at Diablo, got into it with someone from another team. She hauled off and slapped him, and he knocked her down. Ryder popped him in the nose." He smiled weakly. "That's all."

She turned wide eyes on her son, speechless, for once.

Joe turned back to Ryder and shrugged. "We'll just have to step it up a little to make up the slack."

That was the understatement of the year. Dan was the best runner they had. Ryder was good, but Dan was really, really fast.

Then Mom found her voice.

"Ryder, are you all right?" She flew to him and framed his cheeks between her hands, scanning every inch of his face.

He rolled his eyes. They were all that he could move, what with his head in her vise.

"I'm fine, Mom," he squeezed out between pursed lips. "I hit him. He didn't hit me."

Once she'd assured herself her son was okay, she released him and shifted into scolding mode, hands on hips.

"Thank goodness you're not hurt. But what about the woman?" Again she glanced from one man to the other, eager for details. "What on earth could've made her so upset she'd attack Dan?"

Funny, that was precisely what was eating Ryder. He heard again what he'd been trying to unhear ever since last night.

"*St. Pierre thinks the Southside catastrophe's all water under the bridge. That a firefighter's life was expendable—*"

"It's all in that magazine. The one about Napa," Joe said, rising as he took a gulp from his water bottle.

"Gotta bounce—race starts in an hour. Nice to see you, Mrs. McBride. Ry, see you downtown," he said, breezing past them and out the door.

"What exactly did Dan say last night?" asked his mom through clenched teeth.

Ryder sighed. So much for hoping Dan's words would somehow go away.

"Something about Xavier St. Pierre and the Southside Migrant Camp fire."

She hesitated, then flipped open the lid of the kitchen trash and withdrew a brand-new, glossy copy of *Napa Lifestyles*.

"Inside cover. I didn't want Bridget reading it." She gave him a sad, thin-lipped smile.

When Ryder got to the part about Char's father owning the camp, he went as still as stale beer.

Finally, when he got around to inhaling, he couldn't seem to get enough air into his lungs. His head was about to explode with unanswered questions, and it was all he could do not to lose it in front of his mom. But he couldn't go upsetting her further just because he was freaking out inside. He'd grown accustomed to his role as the man in the family.

"Where'd they dig up this stuff, after all this time?"

His mom came around and sat facing him, placing a calming hand on his shoulder.

"Honey, back then, the whole valley was talking about it. It wouldn't have taken much digging. The difference is, now the son of Roland McBride is famous."

Her face was the picture of concern for her son.

"Lord knows, I came close to telling you myself. But I was hoping I wouldn't have to. What was the point? Why dredge up old memories, old hurts? Until you started talking to Chardonnay, it was irrelevant. The fire was a long time ago, and we're recovering, thanks to your acting jobs."

She sat back. "If it weren't for that crazy publicity agent of yours, finagling that invitation to the St. Pierre's party . . ."

Suddenly the cramped little house was suffocating him. He stood, scraping back his chair with a jerk.

"You can't have it both ways, Mom! Don't you see? If it weren't for my acting career, I wouldn't *have* a PR agent!"

He bolted from the kitchen, reaching his bedroom in a few quick strides.

"Ry? Ryder!"

He grabbed his running gear and dashed out the door, leaving his mother wringing her hands on the front porch.

"Good luck in the race, honey!" she called. "Don't forget—I'll be at the twins' baseball game! Call me afterward!"

"Oh—hold on . . ." She ducked back into the house and returned dangling a little bag high in the air. "Your cough drops!"

But he was already jamming the key into the ignition. With a twinge of guilt at his disrespect, he threw it into reverse and backed out of the driveway. There was no time for cough drops this morning.

Chapter 23

Saturday, June 28

A light breeze fluttered Char's racing bib. The birds were singing, the temperature was a balmy sixty-five—not too hot, not too cold—and flowers lined the first stretch of the race route under a milky blue sky. Everything you could want in a race day.

The quinquennial event had created a festival atmosphere in Napa, packing the town with people. Vendors sold food and drinks from trucks and tents. An outdoor yoga class was underway in the park. Athletic gear companies were hawking free samples. A block away where the route looped around to the finish line, a TV satellite truck maneuvered into position.

Today marked a milestone—the achievement of a goal Char had set as a teenager, when she'd first heard of the challenge. For five long years, she'd looked forward to conveying that she was a caring individual with a big heart, not just a spoiled wine heiress. But it was only once she'd narrowed her focus to helping migrant children that she'd found her real passion. For the past six months, she'd geared all her running toward this race. After all the shin splints, all the sweat and the blisters, she was ready to go deep. Go hard for who she'd begun secretly referring to herself as "her" kids: Juan and Amelia and all the others who depended on her small but growing El Valle Avenue mission. Today, of all days, she was supposed to be happy. Excited. So why had she woken up distracted and out of sorts? Until last night, her sole priority had been her new foundation. To that, she was one hundred percent committed. If falling in love had been her goal, last night would've nailed it. Ryder—the man, not the actor—was everything she could ever want in a love match: bright, considerate, sexy . . . with a face that literally stopped traffic and a body to match.

But falling in love with Ryder McBride wasn't part of her plan. In fact, it went against everything she believed.

Because Char wasn't prepared to fall in love with anyone. *Especially* not an actor.

It was no coincidence that she'd never let someone into her life for long. She'd gone out with guys, of course. But whenever they got too close, she backed off before they could reject *her*. Because that's exactly what would happen, as soon as they found out how hopelessly screwed up her family was. Especially Ryder, of all people. Why would *any* guy want Xavier St. Pierre for a father-in-law—even if Papa *weren't* accused of killing his father?

She knew about the accusation before they made love, and she had intentionally hidden that information from him. Had he known, last night might have turned out very differently. But it was only a matter of time until he found out.

Luckily, she had her teammates to rally, keeping her from being completely absorbed in guilt and regret.

Forcing her attention back to the task at hand, she counted heads. Everyone was there. Even Wendy, who seemed to be the only one not affected in the least by what had happened up at Diablo. She was passing the time stretching and chatting.

Char tied her time chip onto her shoelace. Hoping *he'd* come looking for *her*, she forced herself to wait until the very last minute to scan the crowd for Ryder's red jersey. By the time she picked him out, she tried to catch his eye, but he never looked her way. And it was too late to initiate a conversation now anyway. Maybe he'd catch up—rather, fall *back*—with her during the race itself.

At the starting line, she fussed and fidgeted. Then she fidgeted and fussed. Her shoes didn't feel right, her stomach was queasy, and her calves ached. Worst of all, the tenderness between her thighs was a constant reminder of the night before.

Had making love with Ryder been stupid? Yes. Would she do it all over again? In a heartbeat. That's what was so maddening.

At the crack of the pistol she managed to place one foot in front of the other, despite shoes that felt like they were made of concrete.

Within the first quarter mile, three of her fastest teammates rabbited past her without a backward glance, shouting encouragement as they went.

It was only at the second mile marker that Char found her legs. That was when she noticed a skinny boy holding a sign into her path: *¡Corre, Char!* Juan! And with him, Amelia, jumping up and down, and their mother, waving and smiling.

That gave her a boost. When she passed a second-stringer from her field hockey team, a smidgen of her old self-confidence returned.

Pushing hard, she put three more miles behind her. Now her clothes were soaked. She struggled past her goalie and a midfielder who were running as a pair.

Farther down the course, she found her inner forward.

She ripped open a gel pack, squeezed it onto her tongue, and kicked it into high gear.

At that pace, she even forgot about the pain between her legs.

Ryder's lungs were killing him, and he was struggling to shake off the dizziness.

From his calculations, he'd been somewhere among the top third of the men and ahead of most of the women at the eight-mile mark. But every inhalation burned like battery acid.

He wasn't used to limitations. He'd been successful at most everything he'd ever set out to achieve. Then again, he'd never done a half-marathon only two days after sucking on smoke.

At least all of his men were ahead of him, where they still had a chance. Scant consolation, what with Dan on the couch with an ice pack on the bridge of his busted-up nose.

Again, he ran down the mental list of his runners. Was there anyone he'd overlooked who had a remote chance of homering?

It wasn't that his team wasn't strong. Their bunker gear came in at sixty-five pounds, and that was before the mask and air pack. It was just that only Dan and Ryder had any kick in the long haul. The plan all along had been for Dan and Ryder to push for PBs. That was just not going to happen today.

Not that he'd end up roadkill . . . there were still a bunch of guys behind him. But he was going to have to face the fact that, barring some miracle, he wasn't going to finish in the money.

Good-bye, building. And most likely, good-bye, grand prize.

Chapter 24

Now that she'd finally hit her stride, Char wove in, around, and ahead of runners of both genders. At mile-marker twelve, her heart was thundering in her chest, but she had to keep going. The arms and legs of a woman she'd been closely trailing suddenly stiffened up like a toy soldier's. She collapsed to the pavement, and Char veered around her and two white-shirted EMTs that came to her rescue. Poor thing. That's what happened when you hit the wall.

Now Char could see only men ahead.

But that didn't mean there wasn't another female up front, out of sight. Or even on the good side of the finish line.

That's when she saw *him*. His pace was steady, but slow. Way too slow. He should be passing her, not the other way around.

She studied him from behind. Something was clearly off. Without trying to, she was gaining on him. When she came up on him, she registered shock at his appearance. His face was a mask of agony. Deep lines were etched into his forehead. He was practically gulping for every breath.

"Ry. You okay?" she managed to spit out.

He didn't respond. Just kept sucking air.

"Ry."

She reached out and touched his forearm.

"I'm. Fine."

"Your lungs?"

"I said I'm fine." But the effort of saying four words started a spasm of coughing.

She stayed with him, her ambition suddenly forgotten, displaced by concern.

"Don't talk," she ordered.

From the sideline, someone thrust cups of water at them. Ry poured his down his throat, then Char offered him hers. He pushed her hand away, the precious drops splashing uselessly to the blacktop.

The hours of grueling practice that Char had put herself through to get *here* flashed through her head. The ice packs and the heat wraps. The chafing and the sore muscles.

The pain of watching Ryder struggle was worse than all of that put together.

Just as she considered forcibly dragging him off to the nearest first aid tent, he spoke again.

"Go"—he winced—"away! Don't—want—you!"

The knife of his rejection tore into her heart. This wasn't just his pride talking.

He knew. He knew everything.

It was the thing she'd dreaded above all others since she'd been ten years old . . . discarded by her own parents. Back then, she'd only suspected she'd been tossed aside. But this—this was blatant, undisguised rejection.

She had to get away from him. *Now.*

She dug down deep, deeper than she'd ever reached, and she ran.

Away from her hurt. Away from her humiliation. Away from Ryder McBride.

When Meri's lilac streaks came into view, the end was in sight for Char. Savvy was there, too—in black, of course, looking ready for court, even though it was a Saturday.

Char had been watching for her sisters. She'd never dreamed Papa would be there as well.

All three of them leaned out to brush her palm as she sprinted across the finish line. Her shoe chip activated the electronic timer: 60:52:50. One hour, fifty-two minutes, and fifty seconds.

Her EFT—estimated finishing time—was one fifty-nine. She'd bested that by almost seven minutes.

"You won! You're the first woman to cross!" And then her family's arms were around her, surrounding her in a rare group hug.

Meri grabbed a handful of her shirt. "Char! It's you or the fastest guy for the fifty thousand! It's down to just you two!"

"You were amazing," blurted Savvy, pressing a water bottle into her hand. "We're so proud!"

Then there was Papa, his arms outspread. It was too much. She knew he loved her, but he'd never been very touchy-feely. His overt pride was conspicuous to anyone watching. It brought out a buried, childish need for parental approval in Char, and she fell against his chest and burst into tears. His own eyes moist, he kissed her cheeks and raised her arms high, spinning her for everyone to see.

"Chardonnay St. Pierre, *le vainqueur! Zee* winner!" he exclaimed, to cheers and a smattering of applause.

But she hadn't won yet. The overall winner had to be figured out based on the male and female handicaps. They wouldn't find out who'd actually won the money until tonight at the gala.

Someone slipped a medal over her head, snapped a picture, and draped a crinkly foil blanket around her shoulders.

The press stepped in then, jostling her with their intrusive cameras, large and small. "Give her room. Let her breathe!" Meri scolded. But for just this moment, Char didn't mind the attention. For once, she'd earned it.

As they made their way to the hospitality tent, Char noticed a different group hovering around the fringe. They were carrying signs, and their voices were most decidedly *not* congratulatory.

"Poacher!" one of them pointed at Papa.

"Eagle killer!" yelled another.

"Over there!" said a reporter. The TV cameramen who'd been filming Char spun to get an angle of her with the protestors.

Meri and Savvy flew to her side.

"Keep walking toward the tent," said Savvy.

Meanwhile, Papa confronted his foes head-on. "Idiots! What vintner would kill an eagle?" he shouted, hands in the air. "The big birds, they eat the little birds who eat the grapes! I only wanted to scare him away from my fish! "

Char spun around from where her sisters were dragging her across the square, pulling them to an awkward halt when Papa yelled again. He was right in the face of a demonstrator. Jogging toward them were two cops.

Savvy sighed to Meri. "Take Char. I'll go back and handle this."

Char began to tail Savvy, but Meri jerked her back by the arm. "Char! Listen to Savvy. You don't want that."

Char gave in, allowing herself to be led like a child. In the past twenty-four hours she had endured the highest of highs and the lowest of lows. Euphoria, rejection, humiliation, triumph . . . she was beside herself with a combination of endorphins, embarrassment over Papa's old and new exploits, and concern for Ryder's health.

That's when Dr. Simon stepped up to her.

"Chardonnay. Congratulations."

The warmth of her mentor's arms barely registered. She was numb as a zombie.

"I think she needs to sit down," said Meri. "Can someone grab her another bottle of water? Some juice?"

"Can't sit. Need to walk a little . . ."

Distractedly, she looked around. *Where was Ryder?*

When she spied the results board, she slipped through her well-wishers' hands, past their looks of bewilderment toward an official who was busy scribbling times onto the board as rapidly as they came in.

The winning male was a Stephen Fuller, of the Wine Country Community Group.

It all came down to Fuller and her for the bonus money.

Her gaze traveled farther down the list until she found him.

Ryder McBride: DNF.

Did not finish.

"It's a real heartbreaker, isn't it? After all the effort he put into this . . ."

The woman standing at Char's shoulder looked vaguely familiar, if awkward in her designer dress and heels. She and Savvy were the only ones for miles around who weren't wearing athletic gear. She stuck out a manicured hand. "I'm Amy. We met at your party two weeks ago."

Char drew a blank. Her expression must've showed it.

"Amy," the woman repeated, loud and slow, as if to a child. "Ryder's publicist?"

"Where is he?" asked Char. Her voice sounded remote, even to her own ears.

"In that first aid tent."

It was easy to see where Amy was pointing by the crowd surrounding it.

Elbowing past reporters and fans, Char came to an inner circle of Ryder's teammates, some facing outward to fend off those who were trying to get to the movie star–fireman.

When they broke ranks to let her through, she found him lying on a cot. His beautiful brown eyes were closed. An oxygen mask obscured the now-famous nose and mouth.

Ryder cursed his stupid pride. He was an idiot.

He knew better than to attempt this run while he was still recovering from smoke inhalation.

There went fifty k, and there went the new FRF headquarters.

Dammit.

But there was more on his mind than losing the down payment on the building.

He'd known when Char had come upon him during the race that he didn't have a chance. But he hadn't wanted to ruin hers.

He'd seen what she was doing. It was too easy, her staying with him at that pansy-ass pace. She was holding back. No: It was *him* who was holding her back, all because he couldn't catch his breath.

But he'd messed that up, too. When he'd said he didn't want her, what he'd meant to say was that he didn't want her *help*. But he hadn't had enough air to finish the sentence.

Still, why did he even care? The woman was completely bogus, just like Dan said.

Yeah, he was a freakin' genius . . . buying that sweet, innocent act. She was just as self-serving as she accused actors of being.

Char had known full well what Dan had been referring to at the pasta party . . . why he got slapped by her own teammate. And yet she never mentioned a word of it in Ryder's truck, when she was cataloging all her old man's sins.

What were they again? His throbbing head made it hard to think, but the oxygen was helping. It wasn't nearly as bad as it'd been when they'd hauled his sorry ass in here on that stretcher.

Her cousin's a druggie . . . That's right. Her dad has a thing for koi and MAWs. And her mother had deserted her.

Granted, she deserved sympathy for that last one.

Just like he'd deserved to know that it was her son of a bitch "Papa" who—

"Ryder?" asked a female voice.

God damn it.

He shifted the arm he'd tossed across his eyes to shut out the light. When he saw Char standing over him, he let it fall back again.

Next thing he knew an EMT was poking at him.

"How is he?" Char was asking.

"He's been on oxygen about twenty minutes." There was a pause, and then the EMTs voice came again. "How're you doing there, Ryder?"

"Ryder. Talk to me," said Char.

'Talk to me?' Couldn't a guy get any peace around here?

Slowly, deliberately, he sat up. A glance at Char's worried expression made him sigh and run a finger around the mask's elastic strap. He pulled it down over his ears and left it dangling around his neck.

"Let me get this straight, Char. You want *me* to talk to *you*? Seems to me there's some talking you should have been doing last night, before—" He coughed, and the EMT whipped out a blood pressure cuff.

"Maybe you should put the oxygen back on," Char suggested.

Jeezus, would the woman make up her mind? Did she want him to talk to her or put on the damn mask?

"I know. You're right. I was wrong," she said.

Ryder tried to be patient while his pressure was checked, then slipped off the mask completely.

"I'm through with this," he said, handing it to the medic.

"If you say so, boss. Your vitals are strong. Just take it easy getting up."

Char tried to assist when he came rockily to his feet, but he brushed her hand away.

"Ryder. Let me take you to the hospital. A doctor. Something."

"I'm fine. Got an appointment for next week."

He ripped off his racing bib and threw it to the ground as he stalked out of the tent, Char one step behind, reporters bringing up the rear.

"So what is it, Chardonnay?" he bit out. "Tell me. Tell me what you should have told me last night, when you were reciting all of your family's shortcomings. I think you left something out."

She stuttered, but he couldn't control his impatience.

"Is it true? Did your *Papa*"—he spat out the French-accented word with derision—"own that camp?"

"Yes. But he didn't manage it. A management company ran it."

"Oh, so he wasn't in charge. Is that what he told you?"

"Yes . . . he said—"

"You think for one minute he didn't make all the decisions regarding that camp? The maintenance? The living conditions?"

"I . . . I don't know. All I know is what he told me—that it was an accident."

"Well, that's more than I knew."

On second thought, he was through discussing it.

"I'll drop off your car this afternoon."

She jogged to catch up with him. "My car is the least of my concerns. I have an extra set of keys. I'll get one of my sisters to take me up to Diablo. You ought to go straight home and rest."

When they reached his truck, he yanked open his door so abruptly she almost ran into it. The trailing photographers, though keeping a respectable distance, got their angles, crouched, and clicked.

"Ryder, please be careful driving. Where are you going?"

"My brothers' baseball game." He started the engine and rammed it into drive. "From there, Diablo. You'll have your car by one."

"But . . ."

All Ryder wanted was to get the hell out of there. So many disconnected thoughts clogged his pounding head. So many emotions clamored for control of his heart. He needed to sort it all out. But

Char's white knuckles gripped the truck's window ledge like her life depended on keeping it there.

"What about tonight?" she asked, concern etched on her forehead.

"The gala? Do you think you'll feel well enough?"

He checked the time on the dash: eleven oh five.

"Ask me in about eight hours."

He tapped the gas pedal just enough to make her step back. But he'd only rolled a few yards when he braked sharp. Leading with his elbow, he twisted out the window to ask her an important question. When he saw how forlorn she looked standing there, the glacier of his pain melted, but only a degree or two.

"Where'd you place?"

She opened those pretty turned-up lips to speak, but the words caught.

"I—I won."

Chapter 25

Char stared frozenly out the window of Savvy's car during the short drive home, only vaguely aware of her sisters' chatter up front. The stillness of her body belied her emotions, whipping through her like an out of control tilt-a-wheel.

The satisfaction of winning the female division of the race filled a big black hole inside, in a way that no amount of chocolate ever could.

But Ryder's team had lost its chance, partly because of the lingering effects of a brushfire on Ryder's lungs, but also because of a dredged-up story of Papa's involvement in a long-ago migrant camp fire. Angrily, she brushed away the tears that stung her eyes. If there was one thing she should have learned in her turbulent life, it was how to take the bad with the good. Even with all the awful stuff that had happened in the last twenty-four hours—Dan getting punched over Papa's reputation, the pro-eagle protestors stealing the scene at the race, Ryder's DNF—she'd somehow found the stamina to win that race. No one, not the spectators on the side lines—not even her sisters—knew how much psychic energy she'd had to muster to marshal enough physical strength to do that, after everything else she'd been through. That was the kind of deep-rooted power that was invisible. Character wasn't dependent on what anyone else thought. It had nothing to do with having blond hair, blue eyes, and a father worth millions.

She'd always told herself she didn't need a man. Today's victory was proof.

Thank goodness. Because clearly, making love hadn't affected Ryder the way it had affected her. If it had, he should be able to accept anything Papa had done without punishing her, shouldn't he? But no. This morning, he'd destroyed her fragile bliss by shunning her compassion in the middle of the race.

She closed her eyes to try to clear her head. What exactly had she been expecting of Ryder, once he found out about Papa's connection to the migrant camp? Anger? Yes. Recriminations? Of course. But after all that, she'd hoped he would understand her reluctance to ruin their chance at a relationship before it even started.

But to forgive Papa for killing his father? Forgive her for covering it up? If it weren't so serious, it would be laughable. What kind of man could forgive all that?

No one. Not even a movie star–fireman.

Then and there, Char squared her shoulders and resolved to let go.

Last night in the vineyard, she'd made a fool of herself over something as inconsequential as romantic love. She let her guard down this one time and almost got caught. And with an actor, no less! She couldn't let that happen again. Ever. She couldn't afford to put her heart in harm's way again.

At home, back in her room, she changed clothes and made a phone call. She needed to return to her original focal point.

"Bill? I need you. Can you meet me at the El Valle Avenue property?"

"Sure. Let's see here. Will next Tuesday afternoon work? I don't have anything between three and four. . . ."

"Tuesday? Actually, I meant, like, now."

Crickets.

"I—I'm with a client. All the way over on Redwood . . ."

"I'm prepared to make an offer. Today."

Char couldn't put it off any longer. Even if she had to go get a second job and a mortgage in her own name. She couldn't gamble on waiting until next week, when the challenge would be over and Ryder—win or lose—might make off with her building. He might have taken her heart. But she wouldn't let him take her purpose.

"I think I can break away."

"Thanks. Oh, one more thing," she said, remembering her car was still up at Diablo. "Can you stop by my place and pick me up? It's on your way. Just follow Redwood to Dry Creek—"

"I don't need directions," said Bill. "Everybody knows where Domaine St. Pierre is."

All Ryder needed was a nice, long nap. Instead, he dragged himself to the ball field in time to pick up the twins, then stopped at home just long enough for a quick shower before setting out to retrieve Char's car.

He was sapped. But a few days without running or answering fire calls and he'd be good to go.

His mom harangued him about going back out. Then the boys argued like the teenagers they were when they found out Ryder wasn't going to let either of them anywhere near Char's Mercedes.

"Aw, c'mon, Ry! Just let us drive part of the way."

"I'll let you drive my Range Rover next time you come down to LA," he bargained.

"Here," he added, tossing his keys into the air. "Whoever catches these can drive the truck back to Domaine St. Pierre."

The Mercedes was forgotten as the twins tangled for the chance to helm Ryder's beloved old pickup. A surge of gratitude swelled through him. The boys' acceptance of him as a father substitute had gone a long way toward getting them all through the past seven years. He'd be sure to follow up on his promise during their next trip to SoCal.

Brian won the key toss. "You guys know where Char's place is. Take this," he said, handing Ben some cash, "and do me a favor. Stop by that dry cleaner—the one on Trancas—and pick up my tux. Then go get yourselves some sandwiches. Grab one for me, too. I have some business to take care of at Char's winery, but it won't take long. Come get me when you're done."

Ryder hit the button on Char's key fob, and her rose perfume enveloped him as he slid onto the smooth leather seat and started the German engine humming.

A quick glance at the high-tech dash and he was on his way. Highway 29 was an easy shot through the valley, even minus the sedan's superb handling. That gave him ample time to take a closer look around the luxe, cream-colored interior.

From beneath some crisp fliers promoting the challenge peeked something feminine and familiar: the ivory sweater Char had been wearing last night. It was only a scrap of wool, but it awakened something powerful deep inside Ryder. Visions of their lovemaking came rushing back to him. Char's lush mouth. Her dainty breasts. Her voice, calling out his name when they came together.

His fingers itched to touch the sweater that had touched her skin, but something—propriety? good judgment?—kept his hands glued to the steering wheel. That innocent-looking piece of nothingness was more than just a sweater. It was endowed with a magic that sent his thoughts reeling, his blood pumping.

He caved, of course, carefully drawing the material out from under the fliers with his free hand. As he fingered its texture, he noticed the earth-colored smudge tarnishing a cuff.

The recollection of her sweet curves, still so fresh in his mind, tempted him further, and he gathered the material to his nose. The smell of Eden came rushing back, and he closed his eyes as long as he dared while driving, savoring it. When he touched the soft yarn to his cheek, he felt himself rising against his will beneath the steering wheel.

Disgust sent his fingers flying apart as if scalded. The ball of fluff slumped onto his groin. One glimpse of her sweater tenting his hard-on only made things worse.

But curiosity wouldn't leave him alone. Ryder might know Char's body. But he barely knew her mind at all.

What kind of music did she listen to? He touched a button, and his all-time favorite pop station—from way back in high school—came on. Another was programmed to talk radio whose political leanings meshed with his.

Char. If you'd just been honest with me.

But what if she had? What if she'd told him the camp fire was her dad's fault, before she'd taken him on that after-hours tour of the vineyard?

He never would have touched her; that was for damn sure.

Was that what he wanted? Did he really wish last night had never happened?

Chapter 26

Bill Diamond pulled up to the building on El Valle and cut the engine. Char knew he was waiting for her cue, yet she could only sit there zombielike and gaze at it through the windshield while inside her head, her thoughts were spinning at a hundred miles an hour.

"So." Bill sniffed and put his hand on the door handle. "You sure about this?"

She turned deadly serious eyes on him. "Let's do it."

The real question was, *how*? She'd only won the female division of the half. Stephen Fuller, the male winner, could still beat her out of the fifty thou, once they juggled their handicaps. If that happened, the only way Char could honor a signed sales contract on this building was if she won the whole shebang. The whole million dollars.

Just how likely was that? She had no freaking clue. Nobody was allowed to talk about how much they'd raised in donations. She knew how much *she'd* raised to the penny, but she had nothing to compare it to. She'd tried to make a guesstimate, based on past McDaniel Foundation figures that were now public. But the amounts raised varied so much from team to team, year to year, they were practically useless. Throw in the nationwide economic conditions, and who knew how much this year's competition would bring in?

She took a deep breath and blew it out through pursed lips. The very possibility that she, Chardonnay St. Pierre, could actually be hours away from funding her very own foundation was almost too heady to consider. And yet, here she was, taking a gamble on exactly that. Because as far as she knew, Ryder had just as great a chance of winning as she did. And she wasn't going to risk his making a deal tomorrow morning, even if it was a Sunday.

"C'mon," said Bill, opening his car door, putting one foot on the pavement. "Let's take one more spin around the building."

"No," said Char with a stilling hand on his arm.

Slowly he climbed back in.

"Do you have the paperwork?"

Savvy had explained the process to Char earlier. All she needed today was a good-faith deposit—which she would lose, of course, if she reneged on the contract. She and Bill had just come from the bank, where Char had emptied her personal savings account and had a cashier's check drawn up.

"Got it right here," said Bill, reaching between the seats for his briefcase in the back.

"Some things are still done the old-fashioned way—on paper, with a gazillion copies."

He walked her through the contracts page by page, being careful to make sure she understood the considerable financial obligation she was about to commit to, but Char only heard every other word. She'd been through the basics already with Savvy.

"How can I make an offer before I know if I've won?" she'd asked her almost-lawyer sister. "Everyone will know the contest isn't over yet and I don't have the money."

"And everyone will also know that you're the daughter of Xavier St. Pierre. Believe me, you're not a very big risk," she'd said.

"Meaning, they think Papa will make the mortgage payments if I can't?"

Savvy just smiled tightly in ascension. "Of course. Now, I know that's not the plan. You're asking me about the legal aspect, and I'm telling you."

"That's that," Bill was saying when they got to the final page. He handed her his pen. "Sign here."

Without giving it any more thought, Char scribbled her name on the dotted line.

"And here. And here. Aaaaaaaand, *here.*"

Bill gathered the papers together, stuck them back into his briefcase, and started the car.

"I'll call the seller this afternoon, but I don't anticipate any problems. You're offering the whole asking price, and it's been sitting here for over three years. So I'd say it's yours."

Chapter 27

R yder steeled himself as he rang the doorbell of the St. Pierre mansion.

"I'm returning Chardonnay's car," he said to the uniformed housekeeper who opened the door.

For a moment she seemed to think he was some sort of deliveryman. Then, in a flash of recognition, her eyes widened and a smile almost burst her Gallic cheeks.

"*Mais oui!* Hello, Mr. McBride! I saw your movie!" She stepped aside. "Come in. I will tell mademoiselle you are here."

"No, thank you, ma'am. Er, I came to see Mr. St. Pierre."

The woman's smile ebbed, but she nodded him in. "Of course. Please, sit down. I will find him."

The time ticked by. Those were some of the longest minutes of Ryder's life, trapped there in that *Architectural Digest* of a house, waiting for the man who was responsible for—or at the very least, involved in—his father's death.

Restless, he got up and wandered around the elegant room, haunted by Dan's words of warning about the legendary St. Pierres. If Dan were here now, he'd point to this palace as proof that Char's dad was one of the biggest vintners in the valley. It didn't automatically follow that he was crooked, but stack that kind of clout up against the lives of two illegals and a no-name firefighter. If St. Pierre *had* been negligent, what attorney would've mounted a case against him?

Ryder took the edge of his seat again. He rested his elbows on his knees and matched his fingertips together, thinking. Where was the man, anyway? Could be out in the caves or even in the vineyards. Where, coincidentally, Ryder had ravaged his daughter only the night before.

Ryder rubbed his damp palms on his pants. He swallowed, the sides of his throat grinding together like sandpaper.

What was he going to say to the guy when he finally showed up? *Is it your fault that my dad's dead?*

When St. Pierre arrived, Ryder stood, relieved. Anything was better than sitting there waiting, reliving bad memories and dreading the coming showdown.

"Ryder!"

Char's father smelled like cigars and spices. A few short years ago, Ryder wouldn't have recognized St. Pierre's aftershave as several notches above the bug spray that passed for department store colognes. But his time in Hollywood had exposed him to some of life's finer things.

At his side the older man held a faded yellow envelope.

"Such a pleasure to see you again. My apologies for keeping you waiting. I was searching for something to show to you. Come, sit by the pool. We will be more comfortable there."

On the shaded patio, Xavier opened a glass-fronted cooler. "I have wine." He grinned ironically.

It was surreal. Like watching George Hamilton in a TV commercial for wine, pulling a bottle of homegrown from his own cellar. Except that this homegrown went for around a hundred bucks a pop.

"I'll have a glass." It was only midday. But there was a first for everything. Might help his nerves.

Xavier seemed clueless as to why Ryder was there. Apparently, he didn't keep up with the tabloids, either. After ceremoniously cutting off the foil, pulling the cork, and pouring the wine, he inserted his nose into his glass.

"Ahhhh." He inhaled audibly. "Fresh."

Pinching the stem between his index finger and thumb, he tipped it to his lips.

"Sharp and petrolly, with the tang of cat pee."

Ryder's surprised expression made St. Pierre throw back his head with laughter. "Is a good thing."

He looked from Ryder's face to his glass and back expectantly, willing him to drink.

"*D'accord?* You like?"

What could he say? It tasted like white wine.

"Good." Ryder nodded, licking his parched lips.

St. Pierre opened a lacquered box on the side table.

"Cigar?"

More smoke—that's *just* what he needed.

"I'll pass."

"*Bien.*"

Xavier sat back in his thickly padded chair and crossed his linen-clad legs with the air of a man of means.

"First, I will tell you why it is that I cannot speak the good English. People assume I have lived in the United States all of my life, but this is not the case. Of course, I was born in California. But my parents, they were often preoccupied with making the business of wine, here in the valley. So it was better for them if I went away to school in Paris, where we yet have family. When I was finished, I was already eighteen years old. Too late to lose the accent."

Ryder opened his mouth to reply, but St. Pierre held up a halting hand.

"Now. While I am very happy for your visit, I am not so stupid as to think it is for the pleasure of my company. You have been talking to Chardonnay . . ."

Ryder's head jerked up and his eyes locked on St. Pierre's steely gaze for a few pregnant seconds.

"And you would like to know about the fire at the Southside Migrant Camp," he said, calmly lighting his stogie.

The youth that had had to grow up way too fast yearned to jump up and run out of that room, through the huge house, and out the front door, only stopping when he was well off St. Pierre *terroir*. But the man that he'd become kept Ryder firmly planted on his lounge chair. He drained half his glass in one swallow, surprised at how well it quenched his thirst. Maybe he should drink more wine.

"I've waited a long time. Tell me what happened."

Xavier leaned in. "First, I want to say how sorry I am that your father's life was lost in this terrible tragedy. I am looking, but I cannot find the right words to make you understand my compassion. Even though it was seven years ago, it still seems like yesterday to you, no?"

The question didn't need a response.

"I have thought of your family many times," Xavier said, tapping his temple for emphasis. "Please—tell me about them. Then I will tell you the rest."

He refilled their glasses.

When Ryder considered where to start, St. Pierre gave him a prompt.

"How was it that you have become an actor? Is it true what they say . . . that you were discovered by an agent in the church at Yountville?"

Ryder told him how it had all gone down at Saint Joan's, after the mass commemorating the three-year anniversary of Dad's death. Mom and the kids had already left, but Ryder had lingered behind when the agent had approached him with her business card.

Talk about a game changer.

St. Pierre smiled then. "This LA angel. She is Amy, no?"

Ryder nodded. "I think you know what happened after that."

"Yes, well, everybody who loves the films knows the name of Ryder McBride. You are to be commended for your success. As you know, I too am a father, and I can tell you that your papa would be proud of you. *Very* proud. And your family today—they are well?"

"They are. My brothers are in college. My sister's going into middle school."

"And your *maman*?"

He nodded again. "She's good, too. I'm hanging out at home this summer, trying to help her fix up the place. Thanks to the profits from my last film, she'll own it free and clear before long."

"*Encore.* For this, you have my greatest respect."

He sliced the foil off another bottle of wine. Ryder knew it wasn't a good idea, yet when he covered his glass with his palm, St. Pierre appeared to take offense.

"But we must drink to the health of your family."

The cold liquid felt so good—nice and soothing—going down. When that was done, St. Pierre filled their glasses yet again and went over to sit next to him.

"And now I believe it is my turn."

He drew a dramatic breath.

"Today, when the workers come up from the Michoacán, many bring with them their families. They rent the apartments, the houses. Many want the citizenship. Everywhere in the valley, there is great change in the way that migrant workers live.

"Seven years ago, these things were very different. The Southside Migrant Farmworker Camp was only one of many camps created especially for the migrants. As you know, there are thousands of acres here, and not enough men to do the work. It has always been this way. Many single men were coming from Mexico for tilling, tying up the vines, irrigation, and of course to pick the fruit—often by hand. Before the camps, sometimes they were sleeping outdoors . . . in tents . . . anywhere they could find.

"We—some other growers and myself—pooled our resources to provide places for the workers to sleep, to eat. Because they work many hours each day for only a few months, they are only spending nights in these camps before returning south of the border.

"The growers cannot oversee these camps alone, because we must supervise all the tasks that go into the making of the wine, from deciding which grapes to plant through marketing the final product. We hired what is called an ag management company to operate the camps. They provide an on-site manager, housekeeper, maintenance worker, et cetera.

"These camps are like motels. The men who live there are prohibited from cooking in their rooms. There is a separate . . . how do you say . . . *mess hall* for meals. But, as we all know, some people, they do not obey the rules."

Funny that, coming from a man with a reputation for never playing by society's dictates.

"This terrible fire . . . he was an accident." Xavier placed a hand on Ryder's arm, shaking it for emphasis. "A cooking flame that got out of control in the room of the workers who died."

After all the talking, there was an awkward silence while the man eyed him expectantly.

Ryder blinked to clear the blurry edges surrounding St. Pierre's face.

"What do you want me to say? That I swallow your version of what happened, just like that?"

"The insurance company had to do their own investigation. The fire marshal, too—by law. As you know, they are in the business of saving people. They don't like when people die, and they especially detest losing one of their own . . ."

A slight understatement.

"So they were very thorough. The flames from the prohibited cooking stove spread to some extra containers of liquid fuel stored in the room, which caused a number of explosions. The two Mexican pickers died instantly. The blaze spread quickly. It was the middle of the night, and the others were sleeping. By the time the fire department arrived, the whole camp was on fire. Your papa, he became trapped when a wall collapsed as he was saving another man."

Ryder had heard that part of the story, somewhere in time. But with all his more pressing obligations, he hadn't dwelt on it. He couldn't afford to. Or maybe, he'd let his more concrete problems— family, finances—distract him from the pain of imagining his father's last moments. Now, visualizing them, his head dropped to his hands.

St. Pierre picked up the yellow envelope from where it lay on the side table and handed it to Ryder.

"I would like to give to you the reports, for you to read yourself."

With an effort, Ryder raised his head. His headache was coming back with a vengeance. And the wine was clouding his thinking.

He scowled. "How did you know I was coming here today?"

"I kept these, knowing someday you will come. I did not know when."

Ryder reached tentatively for the envelope.

Simultaneously, the door to the house opened. There stood Chardonnay, wearing a white cotton dress and a quizzical expression.

"Papa? What's going on?"

She didn't wait for an answer.

"Ryder, your brothers are in the foyer. They said they expected to hear from you about an hour ago. . . ."

Ryder set the envelope aside, stood, and took a step in her direction. The room spun. He staggered backward, barely catching himself on the chair's arm before landing back in it.

"Ryder!" Char lunged toward him.

That's when the lights went out.

Chapter 28

Ryder slumped back into his chair next to the table holding the empty wine bottles, leaning his head back on the plump padding.

"Papa! What have you done?"

Papa's face was the embodiment of innocence. "*Rien!* I have done nothing but tell Ryder what he came to hear!"

"And what was that?"

"Only the truth!"

Fanning cigar smoke away from her nose, she flew to Ryder and the bottle-strewn end table.

"Did you drink all that wine *today*?"

Her father appeared perfectly sober. But then, he practically drank for a living.

She held up a bottle by its neck and shook it at him. "Three bottles, early on a Saturday afternoon?"

"It is good to drink wine when one is having a serious discussion. It makes the words land easier. . . ."

"But Ryder only has a beer now and then! And today, of all days. He's still recovering from the race. A race he shouldn't even have attempted . . ." She huffed. "Oh, never mind." It was futile, trying to explain simple social concepts to Papa that he should already know.

"I'll bet he didn't even eat lunch," she muttered as she scooped up the other empties and tossed them into the recycling bin. Then she cracked open the door that led from the patio to the house. "Ben! Brian!"

The identical long-legged young men in their slouchy jeans ventured shyly onto the patio, looking somewhat intimidated by their sumptuous surroundings. When they saw their brother passed out on the lounge chair, they started toward him, their wonderment forgotten.

Char downplayed her concern for their benefit. "Don't worry. He's just suffering from exhaustion. Get on either side of him, guys. Let's take him where he can rest a while."

Out of some instinct, she snatched the yellow envelope and led the three McBride brothers through the house, up the wide staircase, and down the hall to her suite, where they lowered Ryder onto her bed.

"He'll be okay. I'll let him sleep awhile, then feed him," she said, herding them out of the room.

Simultaneously, they hesitated, talking over each other. "What are we gonna tell our Mom? She'll be waiting for him. They're going to that thing tonight. She's gettin' her hair done right now."

"Tell your mom to go ahead to the gala. I'll see that he gets there."

While crossing the foyer, one twin braked early and the other bumped into him.

"What about his tux?" asked Ben. Or Brian. She wasn't sure.

Char bit her lip. She hadn't thought of that.

"What he means is, it's hanging in the truck. He just got it cleaned," said Brian. Or Ben.

"It is? Perfect. Why don't you bring it in, so he won't have to run home to change? That'll buy him another hour to rest."

She took possession of the tux and, unexpectedly, a soggy submarine sandwich wrapped in waxed paper. Faking a sunny grin, she waved them off, then dashed to the kitchen for filtered water and a bottle of vitamins. She put them on a tray along with the sandwich and sped back up to her bedroom. Along the hallway leading to Char's suite, the upstairs maid paused, feather duster poised midair.

"Mademoiselle?"

"What, Celine?" She grinned proudly. "You've never seen me carry a tray before?"

Single-mindedly, she flounced by, Celine staring after her.

Char felt good—no—*great*. She always felt her best taking care of others, whether ladling soup, sorting donations, or whatever it took to be a positive force for change.

But this was way more personal. At the moment, her nurturing was centered on one person, not a group of people. Her earlier resolve to forget about Ryder flew out the window. Though he may be unaware of it in his unconscious state, *he needed her*. And she was determined not to let him down.

Ryder was snoring when she got back to her room. She picked up the wrinkled envelope, still lying where she'd dropped it on her nightstand. It was addressed to Papa from an insurance company. The postmark was seven years old, and the flap was hanging open.

Char rifled through the contents, her gaze halting at the names of the fire victims. There it was in black and white: Roland McBride, firefighter, Napa County. Mateo Perez, picker, Michoacán. Gabriel Garza, picker, Napa.

Garza? She frowned. Where had she heard that name before?

She skimmed page after page until she got to what she was looking for, the findings of the fire investigation, exonerating Papa from negligence.

Letting out the breath she didn't realize she'd been holding, she peered down at Ryder, wishing he were awake. Now, with the evidence she held, she was ready to apologize for withholding what little she'd known about the fire before they'd made love. But it would have to be put off a little longer.

In her bathroom, she ran some cool water on a cloth and then returned to lower herself onto the mattress beside him.

"I've learned some things, thanks to you," she whispered, gently wiping his forehead.

"I'll admit it. All actors are not bad. In fact, there's one who's a real treasure. Smart." She kissed his eyelids. "Kind." She cupped his cheek tenderly.

She rambled on, freely voicing every thought that popped into her head. His unconscious condition had a liberating effect on her tongue.

"Not only that, I found out it's true what they say—even negative publicity can sometimes be positive. Did you see those protestors all over Papa today?"

Ryder didn't open an eye.

"Tsk." She shook her head, remembering. "Today was supposed to be our big day—not just mine, Juan's and Amelia's and all the other kids' down on El Valle. I promised them I would do my utmost to win the race so that I could buy them that building. But that's not all. Today was the day I was going to break free from my family's crazy reputation.

"I was thrilled to see Papa there at the finish line, until those angry people showed up with their signs.

"Savvy and Meri don't seem to be as affected by Papa's antics, but he embarrasses me to no end! Don't misunderstand. He's not an awful person. He has a lot of good qualities, and usually he means well. It's true. He did fire a few rounds into the air to scare the birds away from his koi. Those fish are his main hobby. Well"—she chuckled—"that and starlets. But he'd never intentionally harm a flea."

She sighed. "Things just seem to get out of hand when Papa's around. Like this morning. That shouting match between Papa and the protestors ended up getting as much press coverage as the event itself. But the funny thing is"—she stopped wiping Ryder's face, threw her hands in the air, and let them fall to her lap—"after the video hit, our online donations actually soared!"

She laid aside the washcloth.

"Okay, I'll admit—winning the female division of the race might have helped, too. The point is, that video didn't hurt us one bit. I don't know if they were pity donations or what, but who cares? Every dollar helps, right?"

Then she lay down next to him and curled her body close to his. With him there in her bed sleeping, she could pretend that he was hers. Suddenly all her inadequacies faded into the background. Nothing had ever felt more right than being there together with him.

"You know what else I learned today?"

Ryder snuffled and rolled into her warmth.

"That there's something that matters more than what everybody in this valley thinks of me. And that's you."

She lightly kissed his lips.

"You know how I know? Because giving you what you want is

more important than getting what I thought I wanted. I love you, Ryder McBride."

Then and there, Char made a decision.

She would've been content to lie quietly with him until he woke up on his own, but the need to get ready for tonight kept niggling at her. Tossing on her dress wouldn't take long, but her hair and makeup would.

"You just stay here and relax, and I'll be back before you know it," she said, kissing him again, this time on the nose. He smiled in his sleep. Happiness spreading through her, she got up to start to get ready for the gala.

A recurring vibration emanated from the region of Ryder's backside. It was accompanied by a familiar ringing. His hand automatically reached for his back pocket.

"Yeah?" he grunted into his phone.

"Where the hell are you?"

There was only one person on earth whose voice could convey so much venom and sugar in five little words.

"Amy?"

"Who else? What have you been doing? It's five thirty! The gala's in an hour and a half!"

Ryder sat up, rubbing his eyes.

"I have to hand it to you, Ryder. I'd never even heard of this 'challenge' thing, until you got involved. It was never part of my grand promotional plan for you. But now that you're in it, you're committed. You've got to follow through. Tonight's when the winner's announced."

He squinted at his surroundings. Where the hell was he? Looked like the set of some fancy boudoir in an old-time movie—all pink and ruffly.

"Don't tell me about follow-through. Had every intention of going. Still do."

"Then come outside. I'm sitting out here in the limo."

Inside, there was no one else in sight. He now realized that what he was in wasn't just a bedroom—it was more like a suite, with lots of doors. On the wall facing him was a big-ass abstract that reminded him of something he'd once seen at the Getty. Beneath him was a comforter of the softest material imaginable whose subtle print matched that of the drapes on the French doors. Beyond them, he could see a short segment of horizontal wrought iron railing enclosing a balcony that looked out on rolling vineyards.

On an interior doorframe hung a man's dark suit—obvious by its width at the shoulders—in a clear plastic garment bag labeled Trancas Dry Cleaners. His eyes skittered to a tray on the nightstand. Though the waxed paper around the sandwich was crushed and it was sitting in a little pool of liquid, its pungent aroma had him suddenly salivating with hunger. Then it hit him: He hadn't eaten all day.

From another closed door came the sound of a shower running. The third must be the way out.

"Ryder?" asked the voice on the phone.

"I'm coming."

He tossed a handful of vitamin Cs into his mouth, chased them with the water, and grabbing the sandwich in one hand, the tux in the other, exited the bedroom into what resembled the hallway of one of LA's better hotels. He followed it to a marble staircase and down. The rays of late afternoon sun shone through the front doors in exactly the same way they had two weeks ago, on his first visit to Domain St. Pierre. But unlike the night of the party, today the foyer was empty.

Out front, a man hopped out of the driver's seat to swing open the back door of the idling limo.

"You look like shit," grinned the driver admiringly.

"What a coincidence. I *feel* like shit."

The door was shut behind him with a high quality *thunk* as he crawled into a seat opposite his agent. What was so prestigious about limos? It was always so awkward climbing in and out of them.

"You look like shit," Amy remarked.

"I heard."

"What's going on?"

Ryder shook his head to clear it. "Had a few drinks with the old man. Guess I got over-served."

She raised an eyebrow. "In the middle of the afternoon?"

He shrugged. "When in Napa."

"What's done is done," she said, waving it away. "It's not my job to judge. Besides, it's not important that you feel good. All that matters is that you look good."

She was all heart.

"Is that your tux?"

No, it's my pajamas. He gave her a look and rubbed his hand through his bed head.

"Excellent. We're going back to my hotel. You can get ready there." He sat back into the plush leather then. As they pulled onto 29, he gradually became more alert. "How'd you know where to find me?"

"Seriously?" Amy lifted an eyebrow. "It's what I *do.*"

Char wrapped her damp body in a towel and cracked the bathroom door.

"Ryder," she sang happily. "Are you awake? It's five thirty-five. I'll get out of here and let you have your turn."

No reply. He was probably still dozing. She hoped it wouldn't be too hard to rouse him and that his headache wouldn't be too bad after all that booze.

She slathered some moisturizer onto her legs. God, what a day it had been for him! And they still had the gala to get through. She should run downstairs and get him a coffee. She glanced at the time again. She still had to dress and do her hair and makeup.

She called to him again. "Come on in. Get a quick shower. It'll help you wake up."

"Ryder?" She stepped out of the bathroom and looked at the bed. But all she saw was the rumpled comforter and scrunched-up pillows.

"Ry?" She glanced at the nightstand. The sandwich was gone, the cap had been left off the vitamins, and the water glass was half empty.

Char wrapped her towel around her head turban-style, shrugged into a robe, and hurried out into the hall. Could he have gone downstairs? It seemed unlikely that he'd go wandering through the house, but where else could he be? He didn't have a car here. He couldn't have gone far.

Maybe he'd gone to the kitchen. For coffee. Yes, that had to be it.

Good. That was smart. That meant he'd come to and was thinking clearly.

When she reached the top of the staircase, she called for him again. Celine appeared from one of the other bedrooms, carrying an armload of neatly folded sheets.

"He is gone, mademoiselle."

"Gone?" Char repeated. "Where'd he go?"

"In the limo."

She frowned. *"The limo?"*

"With the lady."

"What lady?"

"The same lady he came to the party with."

Amy.

Chapter 29

The limo pulled up to La Maison de la Lune just as Ryder had finished wolfing down his sandwich.

"Ew. That reeks. Here." Before he even knew he needed them, Amy was ready with a distasteful expression and a box of tissues dangling from her thumb and forefinger. But then, that was Amy.

"Thanks." He wiped his hands.

"No need," she said. "That's why they pay me the big bucks."

His stomach felt a little better, now that he'd fed it. But there was a deeper place inside that still felt raw. No wonder he looked so horrific.

They slipped unnoticed into Amy's suite.

"Go ahead and get cleaned up. I'll order a pot of coffee from room service."

A shower felt good, but he couldn't wash away his disappointment in Char.

"Coffee's here," Amy called from the common living room.

Ryder wrapped a towel around his waist and left the bathroom. A little caffeine in his system and he'd be as good as new.

"How you feeling?" she asked.

Maybe she *did* have some warm blood running through those veins.

"Outstanding," he lied.

She handed him a steaming cup.

"Drink this. You'll be fine.

"Like I was saying, it was brilliant, you signing up for this battle of the charities. I've been vacationing in wine country for years. Remember the night I found you, at Saint Joan of Arc? Last night of vacay. And yet, I'd never even heard of the challenge. And this fireman's philanthropic scheme you've wormed your way into is genius. Kudos for finding that all by yourself, too. You're really putting your acting skills to good use."

She poured her own cup and perched herself on the arm of the couch.

"You're getting pretty good at self-promotion. Ever since I introduced you to the St. Pierres, you took the ball and ran with it. I'm sure you've seen the photos. There've been some of you and Chardonnay locking lips, and others showing you running together. Even arguing, after the race. You've done such a good job convincing people you two are a couple, you almost don't need me! That's why I've been giving you a lot of free rein lately. Did you notice?"

Amy's smile was downright wicked. He stared at her, speechless. *Was she kidding?*

"Now, I haven't let go of the reins entirely. Though I did bend my own rules a little, spoon-feeding the Napa press that old camp fire story, but you know how second-rate small town media can be. Once I gave them the headline, though, they jumped on it. That connection between your father and Chardonnay's? Heaven-sent! As they say, you can't make that stuff up!"

Ryder's feet felt like they were glued to the floor, his tongue to the roof of his mouth. Which would be more satisfying once he regained his capacity to move? Tearing Amy limb from limb with his bare hands or letting her incriminate herself even further so he could know the full extent of the damage she'd caused?

She rambled on. "And now, with the challenge intertwined with Chardonnay . . . well, let's just say people will be on the edge of their seats tonight to see who wins.

"So. Listen carefully. Tonight's plan is to get some full-body shots of you with Char. Very *hands-on*, if you get my drift. And keep trying to position yourself between Char and her sisters. Tame is boring. People want juicy. They want provocative—"

But Ryder's tongue had come unstuck. He flagged her with a palm.

"No, Amy, *you* listen to *me*. Do not—I repeat, *do not*—let your paps anywhere near Char again. Not tonight, not ever. Is that clear?"

Amy's face fell. "What? I thought—"

"You thought wrong. You've messed with enough lives with your creepy photographers. I can handle that, but dredging up that story about the fire? That was the limit. How could you be so . . . so . . . callous? People died! My father died. He's dead, Amy."

He turned and started for his room.

"I'm sorry, Ryder, but it was seven years ago. Ancient history—"

He whirled back around. "Try telling my mother that. My little sister and brothers."

Again, he attempted to leave, but she tailed after him.

"Okay, okay. Relax. I can understand how they might still be a little sensitive. But Char? I don't see how it hurts her. She didn't do anything wrong. And neither did her old man, really. He just happened to be a partner in the ownership of the camp where—"

Ryder spun round one last time, his face mere inches from hers. He raised his finger under her nose.

"I mean it, Amy. Do whatever you get paid to do with me. I can take it. But leave my family—and Char—alone. No more stories, no more pictures."

He slammed the door to his room.

But Amy's final words haunted him. Why should he care about Char's feelings? He still resented her for holding back what she knew . . . information that tied them together inexorably. And not in a good way.

The digital clock on the TV caught his eye. His men would be there, at the gala, wondering where he was. And no way was he a quitter. He'd always intended to see this thing through, even though his team's chances at winning were greatly diminished.

It was time to go.

Chapter 30

Scooping up her long skirt, Char strode as fast as she could from her car to the house with the misshapen chain-link fence. The knit fabric was heavier than it looked. Her silver heels were precarious enough without having to dodge the cracks in the sidewalk. Dirt wasn't all she was worried about. Though perfectly apropos for a gala, this high-end outfit made her feel like a Disney princess impersonator down here on dusty El Valle Avenue. But there was no time for a costume change.

The smoky scent of corn tortillas on a hot griddle hit her as she approached the screen door.

How do you keep the urgency out of a knock? She didn't want to panic Juanita, but there was no way she wasn't going to surprise her, showing up on her stoop unannounced in an full-length gown, this time of evening.

While she waited, she composed her face. She had to make this quick to get to the gala by seven, but she couldn't disrespect Juanita by demanding answers to intrusive questions, then blithely dismissing her responses to run off to her charity ball.

"¡Amelia!" Char heard Juanita call to her daughter from the heart of the house. *"Quién está en la puerta?"*

Amelia came to the door and gaped at Char as if she had sprouted wings. *"Senorita Chardonnay, Mamá."*

Juanita's head appeared from around a corner of the dusky kitchen. "One second while I turn the stove off." A second later she was hurrying toward the door—sure enough, brow already furrowed—wiping her hands on a dish towel. When she saw Char's fancy dress and updo, her expression was only slightly less awestruck than Amelia's. She pushed the squeaky door outward. "Come in, come in." With one glance at Char's face, she asked, "What is wrong?"

When Char didn't immediately reply, Juanita ushered her into the tidy, if sparsely decorated, living room.

Should she make a lame attempt at small talk or plunge right in?

"Sit."

Char did as she was told, still clutching her dress in her lap. Juanita took a seat catty-corner, and Amelia perched on its stuffed arm, curious and wide-eyed.

"Nothing is wrong." Char released her armful of fabric to reassure Juanita with a touch. "I won't keep you. You're cooking. It's just—" She struggled for words. "There's something I needed to ask you." She slid her eyes toward Amelia and back. "Grown-up talk."

"Amelia, why don't you show Miss Char your new dress? Go and put it on please."

Char watched the child scamper down the hall.

No more stalling.

"Juanita . . . it's about your husband. What was his name?"

"Gabriel." She frowned. "What is this about?"

"What happened to him?"

Juanita's chin jerked back at the bluntness of her question. "You don't know?"

"I'm not sure. That's what I came to find out."

"It was a fire. Seven years ago."

Char's eyes closed of their own accord. She drew a shaky breath. "Where?"

"At the migrant camp where he was staying. He came here to work, leaving Amelia and me back home in the Michoacán. When Gabriel learned I was pregnant with Juan, he sent for me. He wanted

160 • *Heather Heyford*

us to get a house here, in the US, to be together. It was too hard, living apart. And with another baby coming . . ." Her eyes grew shiny, and she shrugged. "But I was too late. Gabe died before I arrived."

Juan never saw his father.

Juanita blinked and cocked her head, perplexed. "You did not know this? But it was your *papi* that owned the camp."

Char's head dropped to her hands.

When she could speak again, her voice was barely audible. "No. I didn't know about any of it."

Juanita sat back. "But I don't understand. Why then did you help us so much? Why choose the spot across the street for your outreach mission, if you didn't know us, want to make up to us?"

Char's head spun. All this time, Juanita believed she was somehow trying to atone for Papa's sins by bringing donations specifically to Juan and Amelia?

"I wasn't singling anybody out. I want to help *all* the families in this neighborhood. Not just yours." Her eyes bored into Juanita's then as it dawned on her. "It was you who brought them to me, wasn't it? Once you and I became friends, you vouched for me with the others. That's why they came, why they trusted me."

Her friend's guilty smile gave her away.

"But how did you know? How did you know who I was, who my father was?"

Juanita's eyebrows went up. "How many beautiful angels with golden hair and the name Chardonnay are there who drive the Mercedes? I read the papers! I see your pictures." She gifted Char with a fleeting grin before her hand flew to her breast. "Then you also did not know that Ryder's father . . . ?"

"The whole thing was kept from me until very recently," she replied, eyes cast down.

"But Ryder, he knows of the connection? All the names were in the reports—your *papi's*, too. My lawyer showed them to me back then, before I could speak English. When Ryder McBride became this big movie star"—she tapped her temple with her index finger—"I remembered that his father Roland was the one who died with my Gabe."

"What made you stay? Why not return to Mexico, to your family?"

"Juan and Amelia are my family now. Gabe wanted his children to be Americans. To have a fresh start. I bought this house with the insurance money—how else?" She chuckled. "I live frugally. Still, here we are rich, compared to Mexico. We have many friends. We are happy." There was a peaceful wisdom in her soft brown eyes. "You still haven't told me. Why are you coming here asking me this, now, this evening?"

Why was she? She wasn't sure what she was going to do with the information.

"Is Ryder angry with you?"

But Char was still thinking of the Garzas. Meeting the older woman's eyes was one of the hardest things she ever had to do. "I'm so, so sorry, Juanita. For you, and your family. Especially your children. I know what it's like to lose a parent."

Juanita drew a resolute breath and lifted Char's chin with her finger. "You did nothing to be sorry for. And Gabe's *amigo*, the man who started the fire by cooking in *el dormitorio*—er, the bedroom— I forgave him long ago. Mateo was just homesick for his culture. Who knows?" She shrugged. "His English was not so good. Maybe he didn't understand the rules. It is different in Mexico."

"What about Papa?" She had to know.

"Would anger for your *papi* bring back my husband?" Suddenly, Juanita jumped out of her seat. "But wait! Why are you here, when you should be at the gala?"

Of course Juanita knew the ball was tonight. She'd been there to cheer Char on at the race that morning, hadn't she?

"You must go now." She took Char's arm and urged her up, just as Amelia ran into the room in her festive new dress.

"Look. See how fancy she is!" With a change in tone, mother proudly motioned toward daughter.

Amelia twirled, making the wide skirt swish.

Setting her problems aside, Char bent to touch the cotton. "You look gorgeous," she exclaimed.

"And now Miss Char has to go," said Juanita, "or she will be late to the ball. And I have to finish cooking our dinner."

"But—" Char protested.

Juanita led her by the arm toward the door. "Go. Shoo."

Gathering up her hems again, Char turned back from the walk to wave to Amelia and caught a glimpse of Juanita dabbing at her eye with her dish towel, from behind the screen door.

Chapter 31

Everybody in the elegant lobby of the Gold Rush Resort looked up when Char dashed in at seven fifteen, slightly breathless. The jog from the far end of the parking lot wasn't easy in four-inch heels, even for a runner.

Meri and Savvy had been at the resort for hours, taking care of last-minute details on her behalf.

As for Papa, she'd firmly banned him from being within a five-mile radius of the gala.

Papa. She sighed. He was a disaster. Growing grapes was the only thing he did right. Who knew what message Ryder had taken away from their wine-soaked talk?

After her shower, Ryder was gone, the only sign of him a messy bed, an open bottle of vitamins, and the envelope. Not even a note. Not that one was needed. Cutting loose without so much as a good-bye said it all. It was just as she'd told her sisters. Apparently, nothing she or Papa could ever say could atone for his loss.

And now, she had to find a way to live with the knowledge that the Southside Migrant Camp fire had also scarred Juanita and her children.

Juanita said she'd forgiven her, but she'd had seven long years to digest the facts. Seven years to come to grips with her emotions. Maybe, given time, Ryder might be able to give absolution, too. But not many people had it in them to be as gracious as Juanita.

In the meantime, what could Char do with her whipsawed emotions? How could she get through this night?

Compartmentalize. Put all the pieces of her shattered heart in a box and set it on a shelf, to come back to later when she could have a proper breakdown. But it wasn't that easy. Tears kept threatening to overspill her eyes.

Char swallowed the giant lump in her throat and pasted on a smile at some passing acquaintances.

Nothing about this summer had turned out as planned. Even her personal best in the half was tainted by the bar fight that had ruined Ryder's team's chances. If it weren't for Wendy smacking Dan, knocking his team out of the running . . .

No. It had started way before that. If it weren't for Papa, sharing ownership in the camp . . .

She tossed her head, as if doing so could shake her jumbled thoughts into some semblance of order.

If only.

Instead, she summoned the willpower to focus on the cool elegance of the window-lined ballroom, to bring herself back to the present. Soon it would be dark outside, and the panoramic exterior view of manicured grounds would contract to the details of its chocolate brown interior.

White-clothed tables were piled with a stunning array of auction items collected by the contest participants. From across the room, Char watched Meri put the final touches on her artistic vision, turning Char's donations into a sensational-looking spread. Just as Char had imagined, there were the colorful baskets overflowing with fruits and vegetables, tied up in bows. Sparkling wine bottles nestled in straw-lined wood boxes. All the gift certificates had been framed in silver, then set on easels. And Meri's one-of-a-kind necklace sat mounted on black velvet.

She wove through the tables to her sister. "Meri, you've outdone yourself. I can't thank you enough. The jewelry, the displays . . ."

A quartet brushed by Char, openly scrutinizing her Grecian goddess gown paired with Meri's gold chandelier earrings, as they offered their congratulations for winning the half.

"Ever have the feeling you're in a zoo?" whispered Meri.

"They're looking at you, too, you know. It comes with the *terroir*." Their names and faces had attracted the spotlight even before all the buzz about Char and Ryder started. That couldn't be helped; it had always been that way. And granted, the race had earned Char even more recognition. That was fine, too. She'd worked hard for that.

What wasn't fine was notoriety for its own sake. Char had never asked to be a rock star. If people admired her, let it be because she wanted to help those less fortunate. Or because she was a tough competitor on the athletic field. But not because her father was rich or because she'd been seen hanging around town with this year's Mr. Napa—kissing, running in skimpy shorts, even arguing in public. She'd only been back in town a month, and instead of improving her reputation, she'd made it worse. How could she blame anyone for believing she was just another branch of the most off-the-chain family tree in the valley?

None of it would've mattered, though, if Ryder cared for her as deeply as she did him. His acceptance was all the approval she needed. But the chances of that happening were close to nil now. It was useless to dwell on it.

How had she ever, even for one day, been brash enough to dream she could have it all: a stable family, romantic love, and the chance to give back?

Papa was out of control. Her chance at romantic love was ruined. Now, all her hopes rested on one last thing, the only dream she had left: her professional goal of helping others. The grand prize.

Ryder held the lobby door for Amy as Xavier St. Pierre's black limo pulled under the awning of the resort entrance.

Xavier stepped out himself while his driver dashed out to get the door for his companion. "Ryder! *Une seconde.* I would like a word with you."

Ryder froze. Now what? And who the hell was that young chickadee with St. Pierre? Miranda? *Jeezus.* She must be a third of his age. How much weirder could this day get?

Amy looked back. "Miranda, isn't it? Why don't we go inside?" she said, extending a hand to her. "Let them talk."

Sometimes Amy Smart actually lived up to her name. To Miranda's questioning look, Xavier gave a curt nod. She swept by Ryder with a flirtatious smile before disappearing through the door, Amy close behind.

"My daughter scolded me after our little talk this afternoon," said St. Pierre, peering down his nose. "She said I gave you too much wine."

You did. Still, Ryder took responsibility for his own actions. He was a man. He should've exercised more self-control.

"Do you remember the things that I told you?"

Some. "Which things, in particular?"

"About the fire. The camp."

Disjointed fragments. An illegal cookstove. Extra fuel sitting around. A yellow envelope. Ryder was having a hard time piecing them all together.

"If you remember anything, remember this. Nothing we talked of is the fault of Chardonnay. She was an innocent child when it happened. Seventeen. In school, in the east. So please, if you must blame someone, blame me. Do not punish my daughter."

He started toward the door, then paused.

"Read the reports. It's all there."

Char had just sat down at the table reserved for her team when she caught movement near the double doors across the ballroom. She looked up, and in walked a radiant Ryder McBride. If he felt anywhere near as good as he looked, his nap had done wonders. A million watts of electricity ricocheted through the room. Tablemates nudged and whispered. Necks craned, heads dodging left and right to get a better view of Napa's biggest star.

More tuxes and flashy gowns materialized, packing into the space until it vibrated with movement and conversation. Men reached out to slap Ryder's back or shake his hand. Moon-eyed women stood on their tiptoes to touch their cheeks to his in air-kisses. If Char thought she'd ever been the center of attention, that was nothing compared to the stir he was causing. But unlike her, Ryder seemed to take it all in stride, as he made his way to his team table.

She wished she could be more like him, accept celebrity with aplomb. But then, why shouldn't he? Ryder had nothing to be ashamed of. *His* mother hadn't abandoned his family to run off with a strange man and died in a car crash. *His* father wasn't a serial philanderer. And as far as she knew, no one in his family had ever done time. Ryder got attention for all the right reasons, whereas she, on the other hand . . .

Char forced her gaze away. She looked down at the table without seeing the gold-banded china and massive floral centerpiece. Her mouth was dry as the desert. She reached for her water glass, but she could only choke down the tiniest sip. Then she sensed his presence grow stronger, drawing her like a magnet. Her heart pounded, the roaring in her ears drowning out the buzz of conversation. She fought and lost a powerful urge to look up again, and there he was, mere feet from her. Her eyes sank into his, her breath coming fast and shallow. When she'd had him on her bed just hours ago, wasted, she'd bared her soul to him. Her face warmed, remembering. She'd told him she loved him. Did he care? Had he heard a word she said?

Ryder maintained steady eye contact with Char even as he leaned over to listen to a seated woman in a red dress whose hand held his forearm captive. This close, Char saw a certain sadness beneath his public smile. The longer he looked into her eyes, the blacker his pupils grew, till they eclipsed all their hazel color. Char's burning eyes blinked first, and just that quick, someone was taking his other arm and pointing to a distant table, and he allowed himself to be led away.

He didn't want anything more to do with her. He couldn't have said it louder if he'd shouted it from the podium.

It seemed like forever until the waiter came to clear the plates in preparation for the live auction.

"Was your meal all right?" he asked. "Looks like you barely touched your food."

"Just nerves." She managed to maneuver her lips into a polite smile.

"I understand. Anxious for the outcome of the contest," he said, swooping her plate away.

The majority of the auction articles were part of the silent bidding. Before dinner, bidders had written their best offers down on a slip of paper next to the displayed item. That part was over now, and the winning bids were being tallied behind the scenes.

Next on the agenda was the live auction. Only a few of the more extravagant items—trips, spa stays, and the like—were included in that. An FRF-donated helicopter tour of the wine country roused a lively bidding war, and Char's stay at a well-known Yountville bed-and-breakfast drew a good price, too.

Then the music began again for dancing, while the McDaniel Foundation staff added up all the money.

"I brought you something." Meri plopped down next to her with a plate. "Chocolate mousse." She strained to be heard over the orchestra.

Char shot her a questioning glance. "Dessert has already been passed out. White cake with strawberry filling."

"I went back to the kitchen and pleaded a strawberry allergy." Meri winked.

What would she do without her sisters? Char picked at her mousse with her spoon. She didn't want to seem unappreciative, but under the circumstances, she couldn't even stomach her favorite food.

Even so, she forced down another bite. Anything to distract her from the random glimpses of Ryder she'd been catching on the dance floor. No one had asked her to dance—not that she wanted to. All she wanted was for this night to be over.

She checked the time on her phone to see it was only ten minutes later than the last time she'd looked. She sighed. Counting up the money was taking forever.

And then, finally, the end drew near. Dr. Nicole Simon took the podium, and the music stopped.

The atmosphere was supercharged. Everyone was out of their seats, in anticipation of the results. Even the waitstaff had come out from the kitchen, hugging the walls to be among the first to hear who won the challenge.

Char blew on her freezing hands, until Meri took one and Savvy grasped the other.

Dr. Simon's opening remarks barely registered on Char's ears. It wasn't until she got to the important part that Char started paying attention.

"I have the winner of the half-marathon, based on the handicaps. As you know, the individual prize is fifty thousand dollars."

Nicole fumbled with the envelope.

"And the winner is: Stephen Fuller of the Wine Country Community Group."

Char's supporters sent her sympathetic smiles. She joined in the applause for Stephen when he went up to accept his award.

"There's still the grand prize," whispered Meri in her ear.

Char smiled wanly. All she was waiting for now was the chance to congratulate the big winner and slip off quietly into the night. She'd already begun racking her brain for alternative funding options for her foundation.

"And now, ladies and gentlemen, the news we've all been waiting for: the winner of the challenge and one million dollars."

Dr. Simon paused for effect.

Char's sisters captured her hands once more and clenched them tight enough to break the bones in her fingers. Meri, the youngest, shimmied in her excitement.

"While this year's winner is a first-timer in our contest, its founder is an experienced fund-raiser and volunteer. This person has ladled soup, washed and folded donated clothing, and swept floors at a homeless shelter. Five years ago, this individual came to me and told me she intended to participate in the next challenge. She was only an ambitious teenager at the time, and I wouldn't have thought any less of her if she'd recanted. But in the intervening years, she earned a degree in public service from the University of Connecticut . . ."

But Char didn't hear what came next, because Meri was squealing and Savvy had a death grip on her arms, and then her whole team was on top of her, jumping up and down, whooping and yelling. Dr. Simon raised her voice to be heard, and as Char's full name was broadcast, the entire room erupted.

After all the ups and downs of the past forty-eight hours, Char thought she might burst. While her mouth bowed in a huge grin, her chest heaved, as one after another of her family, friends, and teammates embraced and congratulated her before passing her like a soggy beach ball toward the stage to collect her prize.

Papa appeared from out of nowhere, disobedient as usual, but for the first time, she was glad. The fact that Miranda was draped across his arm didn't even faze her, what with everything else she was attempting to absorb.

"I could not abandon you. Not again," he said, his expression more poignant than she'd ever seen it. "Never again." He kissed both her wet cheeks.

How much more could a girl take?

Papa steered her to the base of the stage steps.

Char gazed up to where Dr. Simon glowed with dignified pride.

Lifting her dress, she picked out the steps in her towering heels and glided to the mike. From up there, the applause sounded deafening.

Somehow, the content of her speech took precedence over her emotions. She thanked her family, her team, and her contributors, and then took advantage of those crowded around to lay out her plan for her foundation.

"Chardonnay's Children are truly the children of the vineyards. They are the sons and daughters of immigrants. These children are, in a sense, victims, here through no fault of their own. In many cases, they suffer from fear, isolation due to language barriers, an achievement gap, and poor housing options.

"Here in Napa County, only twenty-two percent of Latinos go on to college, versus forty-two percent of Anglos. My foundation will educate parents on the importance of education, fund ESL and civics teachers at our new after-school center, and encourage community involvement to lessen isolation. We will also work for more affordable housing. And this is only the beginning.

"But immigrants are not the only ones who need our help. There is no shortage of suffering in our county or of victims."

Where had that statement come from? That wasn't part of her prepared speech. From her spot on the dais, she glimpsed Meri and Savvy exchange an "uh-oh" look.

Char dug down deep and found an inner well she hadn't known existed. She waited for the confused murmuring to die down. Finally, she knew what had to be said to let the healing begin. *Her* healing. She couldn't control anyone else.

"While all of the worthy organizations represented here tonight deserve our admiration and support, there is one particular cause that is close to my heart. That cause is fire prevention and victim assistance."

From the epicenter of the room, Ryder's line of vision found hers. He shook his head and mouthed the word *no*. Instinctively she knew: He didn't want her to squander her moment in the spotlight on him. She tore her eyes away from his. If she didn't, she wouldn't be able to go on.

"In some ways, our causes overlap. Half of all the people who die in fires had no smoke alarms, despite semiannual public service announcements to install fresh batteries. But these reminders only work if people understand the language they are given in.

"Yet there is another, more personal reason that this cause is so important to me. And that is because of my connection to some very special friends.

"Seven years ago, my father owned an immigrant worker camp. It was built to give farmworkers—hardworking men, far from home—a safe place to sleep and to eat."

The buzz began again, down on the ballroom floor.

"Though that camp may seem inadequate now, it was a product of its time. Despite responsible oversight, and to the everlasting regret of my entire family, the Southside Migrant Farmworker Camp was the site of a tragic, accidental explosion in which two migrant workers and one firefighter lost their lives."

The crowd hushed in disbelief that the ugly, open secret would be dragged out here, in this high-class setting, with Xavier St. Pierre in attendance—and by his own flesh and blood.

"I am not here to make excuses. But it wouldn't be right if I didn't take this opportunity to honor the memory of the men who died that night. Their names are Mateo Perez, Gabriel Garza, and Roland McBride."

A tentative smattering of applause reached her from dark pockets of the room. And then she spotted movement. The crowd, parting to make way for Ryder, weaving toward the stage. Toward her.

As mysteriously as it had arrived, Char's self-assurance crumbled, stranding her there on quaking knees with a trembling lower lip, exposed before the eyes of the entire Napa Valley. With Ryder's every step, the applause swelled.

He leaped onto the stage. Like a movie in slow motion, he strode toward her. She no longer heard the ongoing sound of clapping. Of the hundreds of faces in the room, the only face she saw was his.

When he reached her, he took a moment. But it wasn't a put-on. It was *real*. Ryder McBride acted as though they were the only two people in that room. Because to him, they were.

Finally, he pulled her into his embrace. He rocked her back and forth while she released pent-up tears of regret and desolation. Filled her up again with love . . . hope . . . redemption.

Suddenly she could hear again. The earlier cheers were eclipsed by the current bedlam. His embrace and the uproar of approval seemed like they would go on forever.

At stage right, Dr. Simon attempted to fan away her emotions. And then up climbed the others. Papa. Her sisters and Ryder's family. And dozens more, flooding the stage, all wanting to get close to her and Ryder, to be part of their reconciliation.

Over the heads of the crowd, a designer-clothed arm waved like that of a film director and Amy's voice could be heard above the din, supervising some unseen photographer. "Are you getting this? Do we have video? I want video!"

Chapter 32

10:10 p.m.
Thirty-two retweets

AmySmartPR @AmySmartPR 10m

@ChardonnayStPierre wins #NapaCharityChallenge, reconciles with @RyderMcBride in massive group hug @NapaUnbound @GouldEntertainment

Chapter 33

"This could be dangerous," said Ryder, nuzzling the point of Char's breast.

When she leaned back from straddling him, his dad's old wheeled desk chair rolled a few inches, throwing her off-balance. She gasped and he tightened his grip on her hips.

"See what I mean? What is it you have against plain old beds?" he asked.

"You'd better back off on the first responder training. You're almost too safety conscious. What is it you have against chairs?" she countered.

"And vineyards?" He began counting on his fingers. "And pickup trucks? And—"

She interrupted him. "Okay, I get it. Fine. If that's the way you want it, we'll only do it in bed, once a week on Saturday nights with the lights off." She smiled coyly. "Is that what you want, Chief McBride?"

His smile faded.

"What's the matter? You look disappointed." She faked a pout.

Quick as a flash, he turned her over his knee and gave her rear end a swat through her jeans.

"Stop!" she squealed, kicking, her laughter ringing off the concrete block walls of her building, where for the past two months they'd been supervising renovations and scrounging for secondhand office furniture together.

She heard a knock.

"Stop! No, really, stop!" She jumped up and yanked down her shirt. "I heard someone!"

Then they both heard it. Ryder hopped up, too.

"Someone's at the door."

Still giggling, Char peeked around the corner of the office to see a little boy's nose pressed up against one of the front windows.

"That's Juan! And Juanita and Amelia! Look, they're loaded down with stuff. I'll get the door. You help her with the bags."

She hurried to let them in.

Ryder took one of the bags, and Char followed them over to the brand-new kitchen, where Juanita began unloading, stocking the cabinets and the fridge.

Ryder held up a jar of homemade salsa. "What time's supper?" he asked, making a show of rubbing his stomach.

"You go," Juanita said, shooing him away with her dish towel. "Go away. Let me cook."

"Yes, ma'am," said Ryder, dodging her aim.

"I will call you when is supper."

"C'mon, Juan. How'd you like to shoot a little hoops while your mom's cooking?"

"Yeah!" shouted the little boy.

Char took Amelia's hand, and they followed them out to the newly fenced and lined basketball court. While they watched, another car pulled up and parallel parked, and out came Lori MacKenzie and her son Jimmy. Ryder yelled for the boy to join him and Juan on the court.

"How's it going?" asked Lori. Char had met the MacKenzies at Ryder's mom's house, soon after the challenge. The McBrides were good friends with the MacKenzies.

"Almost finished. They're painting the trim starting tomorrow, then your new offices should be all ready."

"I can't wait," said Lori. "I don't mind working at the market, but the hours are killing me. I want to be home with the kids in the evenings and on the weekends. Jamie's technically old enough to watch Jimmy, but still . . ."

"Ryder feels lucky to have you taking care of things for the FRF. It'll be nice. Even when Jimmy's off from school, he can be here with you, on the playground, or playing games inside. And I'll be glad to have you and Juanita around to keep me company while I'm here running the Chardonnay's Children side of the building."

"Lucky for me I have an office background from my previous job. I just hadn't found anything in my field since James died, what with the recession and all."

"By the way, has he made a decision?" Lori asked, lower so Ryder couldn't overhear.

"About moving back to LA after this film wraps? Yes," Char said, feeling her cheeks warm and a smile tighten her cheeks.

"Well?" Lori asked.

In reply, Char held out her left hand.

"Oooooooh!" Lori squealed and grabbed Char's fingers. "Oh my gosh! Oh, I bet his mom is thrilled. She's always been a fan of yours, you know. And Bridget! She's gotta be over the moon! When's the wedding?"

Char shrugged. "We don't know. He just gave me the ring over the weekend. But he has decided one thing: He's going to take a break from acting. Now that he's getting paid for *First Responder, Triple Play's* almost finished shooting, and the FRF is settled in their lease here, he wants to take the winter and fix up his mom's place. Then— and this is so exciting!—he's enrolled in San Jose State for the spring semester."

Lori's jaw dropped even lower than when she'd seen Char's ring. "You're kidding! Ryder McBride, going back to college?"

"It's what he's always wanted. He quit after his junior year to help out his family, you know. . . ." Char left the rest of the story unsaid. Lori knew all about Ryder's family. She and Ryder's mom had grown super close since both their spouses had been killed in the line of duty.

"Anyway, Ryder thought he'd take some time off acting. Doesn't mean he won't read some interesting scripts if they come his way. He's just in no hurry to jump into the next big thing."

Ryder left the boys chasing after balls on the court and sauntered over to the women.

"Congratulations." Lori hugged him.

"Thanks," replied Ryder. He draped an arm around Char's shoulder. It was the kind of small gesture that made her feel so loved. She'd never take that feeling for granted.

"Hear you're going to start cracking the books again. Better keep an eye on him, Char. All those young girls down at San Jose State . . ."

"Young girls? It's the older ones I'm worried about. His humanities prof is already gaga over him," said Char, giving Ryder a sidelong glance.

"I'll share Dr. Simon with you," said Ryder.

"Promise?"

"I promise, hellcat," he said. He pulled her to him in a one-armed hug. "That your phone vibrating?"

He released her, and she drew her cell from her back pocket. "Hey, Meri."

"Char?" Meri sounded frenzied.

"That Realtor friend of yours—Bill Diamond? He's a genius. A little outspoken, but a genius. We spent the whole day together. You won't believe what I did. Papa's going to fart a crowbar."

Char sighed.

A stable family, romance, and the chance to give back. She'd settle for two out of three.

Rapid-fire Q&A with Heather Heyford

1. What brings you the greatest joy?

   Two things: working toward goals and beautiful surroundings.

2. Do you and your husband have a song?

   Yes. It's *99 Problems* by Jay-Z.

3. For whom do you have the most compassion?

   Children and animals.

4. What is your pet peeve?

   Bad grammar.

5. What talent do you wish you had?

   Singing

6. Who would you most like to have dinner with?

   Anyone smart with a loud laugh.

Celebrate the California Crush at Home with a Chardonnay Tasting!

Given all the tourists, no wonder harvest time in wine country is called the crush. But who says you have to be in Napa to celebrate? Here's what my cousin Jamie and her husband Chef Gerry cooked up for my *A Taste of Chardonnay* launch party. Gerry's warm pumpkin soup proved every bit as popular as my book. Here I'm adding my own fancy-sounding, but simple sandwich. Toss in grapes and sliced fruit, and you have enough for a brunch or supper.

Menu: Your choice of California chardonnays for tasting, Warm Pumpkin Soup, Croque Monsieur, mixed nuts, fruit platter

Warm Pumpkin Soup

1 yellow onion, minced
2 Tbs. olive oil
1 29-oz. can of pumpkin
2 (14.5-oz.) cans of chicken broth (4 cups)
½ c. heavy cream
2 tsp. pumpkin pie spice
1 tsp. salt

Sauté onion in olive oil over low-medium heat until soft (do not brown). Stir in pumpkin, broth, cream, pumpkin pie spice, and salt. Stir and bring to a simmer. Serves 4 (8 cups).

Croque Monsieur Sandwiches

1 French baguette
12 oz. Gruyere, grated
Dijon mustard
8 oz. sliced ham (optional)
butter
fresh sprouts (optional)
nutmeg

Cut the baguette into fourths, then slice open each fourth. Spread the exteriors generously with butter, then spread the interiors lightly with Dijon mustard. Layer on the ham, then the cheese. Dust very lightly with nutmeg. Top off with fresh sprouts. Close sandwiches and cook in either an electric panini press or in a heavy skillet, pressing down on sandwiches with a spatula until the cheese is melted and the exteriors are golden brown. Serves 4 as sandwiches, or more if cut into appetizer-size pieces after cooking.

The St. Pierre sisters have been through a lot, but they never expected a bombshell like this. Keep reading to discover what happens when the trio finds out there's a fourth!

A TASTE OF SAKE
Available Fall 2015

In the vineyard under a pergola dripping with wisteria, the priest smiled and said, "Please hold hands."

'The farm boy and the heiress.' That was the phrase whispered among the out-of-towners during the long wait for the ceremony to begin.

And that's exactly what it looked like on the surface . . . groom's deltoids threatening to bust the shoulder seams of his suit, bride the epitome of elegance, auburn hair pulled back to accent her oval face.

The reality was a little more complicated. True, the bride had been born into one of California's wealthiest wine families. But when it came to substance . . . character—call it what you will—the Moraleses had it all over the St. Pierres. Every Napan here knew it, but not one dared utter it out loud.

When Bill Diamond got the phone call inviting him to the Domaine St. Pierre estate on this late June afternoon, he had no idea what it was all about. Figured it was one of Xavier St. Pierre's summer galas . . . the high point of the summer social calendar. As real estate agent to Chardonnay and Merlot St. Pierre, Bill had been mildly pleased to find he'd made the guest list.

Then to find out that this was a wedding—of St. Pierre's oldest daughter, no less? Even cooler. Bill didn't even mind the delay in the start of the ceremony. How could anyone complain, when St. Pierre kept the wine flowing freely? Bill passed the time making new acquaintances. No such thing as a shy successful Realtor.

St. Pierre knew how to throw a party, that's for sure. Star-studded crowd, flowers everywhere you looked. Live music and butlered hors d'oeuvres passed before the ceremony. Even an altar made out of a wine barrel. Then again, what else would you expect from Xavier St. Pierre?

Bill was seated in the second row on the bride's side of the aisle. The lady with the big pink hat in the front row must be a close family friend. St. Pierre's wife was gone, killed years ago in a car accident. Everyone said those girls had it all, but they forgot they'd grown up without a mom.

The music stopped. The wedding party was in position, under the pergola. Game time. So why wasn't Savvy mooning back at Esteban during this special moment? Why was she peering out into the distance, her smooth brow pinched with concern?

A faint *chug-chug-chug* entered into Bill's consciousness. He'd filtered it out until then, to focus on the spectacle a few yards away. Now he looked in the direction of the sound, up and to the left. That's when he saw the chopper, the size of an acorn, coming up from the south.

No big deal. Any second its course would take it veering away.

But as the seconds passed, instead of veering away it seemed to be making a bee-line for the winery. When even the groom swiveled his head around to look, polite twittering rippled through the crowd.

The priest was going on about love and trust and how marriage was a sacred oath. Bill couldn't be sure, because now the noise from the chopper distracted from his voice.

Undaunted, the priest cranked up the volume. "Esteban Morales, do you take this woman to be your lawful wedded wife, to have and to hold—"

Esteban interrupted him. "I do," he said, loud and clear. Following another backward glance, Esteban's right foot turned almost imperceptibly in the direction of the sheltering mansion.

The murmuring grew into nervous laughter. Bill kept a discreet eye on the helicopter. Around him, a head turned here, a chin pointed there. Something about the chopper's trajectory didn't seem right. It wasn't flying in a straight line, or at a consistent altitude. It swung from side to side, rising and falling at random.

"Sauvignon St. Pierre, do you take this man to be your lawfully wedded hus—"

"I do!" Bill saw her lips move but he couldn't hear her soft voice at all above the racket.

Now the foreboding was chilling, palpable. The helicopter drew closer and closer, larger and larger, threatening the party like a big-eyed bug.

It shouldn't be rocking like that—as if the pilot were drunk at the controls.

Was he actually going to bring it down here? Right here, in the middle of the wedding?

The tall cypress trees surrounding the estate swayed and pitched. Looking at the sky, the priest yelled as loud as he could. "Thenbythe-powerinvestedinmebythe ChurchofAlmightyGodandtheStateofCali-forniaIherebypronouceyoumanandwife. *Run!*"

Shit just got real. The groom grabbed his bride's arm and tugged toward the protection of the house, but Savvy's feet were rooted to the grass, her mouth hanging open in horror. Not wasting a second he swept her up—piece of cake for a man of his size—and took off at a tear.

"Go!" shouted Bill, hand on the back of the man standing next to him. Women screamed and men yelled under the now-deafening machine-gun drone of the chopper.

"He's coming down!"

"Get out of the way!"

Chairs toppled like bowling pins. One heavy woman was knocked to the ground by another terrified guest. Bill stopped and yanked her up by the arm.

"He's not going to make it!" somebody cried.

"Get up!" yelled Bill to the woman. *"Come on!"*

The woman winced in pain. *"I can't! My ankle!"*

Thanks only to adrenaline, he was able to haul her to her feet. "Put your arm around my waist!"

Burdening himself with her was going to be the death of him, but he couldn't just run away and leave her to burn up in the imminent fireball.

"It's going to crash!" said the lady in a wobbly voice, some perverted fascination making her look back, slowing them up even more.

Bill jerked her onward toward an outbuilding. "Keep going! Don't look back!"

This was happening.

Bill managed to get her around the back of the shed, where she melted onto the grass. It wasn't much in the way of shelter but it was the nearest structure. Ignoring his own advice, he peered around the corner. Directly above the altar, the helicopter's engine sputtered, died, revived and sputtered again. It shuddered and swung in mid-air for a surreal moment, like a puppet on a string.

Bill crouched and covered his head with this arms, steeling himself for the impact.

There was a dull thud, a sharp crack, and an earthshaking jolt beneath his feet.

Next to him, the woman whimpered.

And then there was only the sound of the cypress branches, swooshing softly back into place.

Bill peeked around the corner of the shed. The lawn was in a shambles. Chairs upended, a portion of the pergola sagging all the way to the ground, floral arrangements broken apart and scattered. In the middle of it all sat Xavier St. Pierre's helicopter, tilting sharply to the left.

The rotors were still. There was no smoke, no fire. No twisted metal.

From somewhere in the distance came a faint sob. From somewhere else, a masculine voice intoned, *call 911.*

Gradually, the surroundings came back to life. Guests crept tentatively out of the far corners of the winery grounds and buildings, brushing themselves off, retrieving lost hats and heels.

Esteban Morales sprinted from the mansion to the crash site, followed by his wife, ignoring his shouted plea to stay back.

Merlot dashed out of the building housing the blending lab, into the arms of her relieved boyfriend.

"You okay?" Bill asked the trembling woman next to him. At her nod, he jogged toward the wreckage to see if he could be of assistance.

The chopper's left landing skid lay some distance away, snapped off in the impact, which explained why the cabin was leaning so hard. But wait—there was movement behind the reflective windscreen. The pilot's door cracked open.

Out on Dry Creek Road, a siren wailed.

And then Xavier St. Pierre climbed out, ducked beneath the blades, and waved to Bill and the stunned semicircle of onlookers that was accumulating.

"Bon après-midi!" he called, zipping around the chopper to the other side.

He yanked on his passenger's door. Its bottom edge ripped into the lawn, building a dam of dirt. Using both hands this time, he yanked again.

Bill gestured to the others. "C'mon, help me prop it up." He and a few men pushed the chopper upright, holding it there until Xavier got the door open.

Onto the lawn fell a female with long black hair.

Carefully, they set the chopper back down.

Savvy and her sisters ventured closer to the victim. Everyone knew St. Pierre was a player. Was this his latest fling? The poor girl lay face down, unmoving. Was she hurt?

"Is there a doctor here? A nurse?" called Bill. Now would be a good time for one to step up. But all he saw was a wall of St. Pierre's cronies—vintners, politicians, entertainers—staring back at him. None of them were any better equipped than a Realtor when it came to caring for a plane crash victim.

His gaze swung back to the passenger on the ground.

"Don't touch her," yelled a woman on the fringe, cell phone glued to her ear. "There's an ambulance on its way."

Bill crouched and gently lifted the girl's hair from her face. "Are you okay?"

Just then a terrier-like object flew out of the helicopter, scrabbling up next to the girl. He barred his teeth and growled, revealing a prominent under-bite.

Bill held out a hand. "Easy, boy."

The dog whimpered, licked his chops, and panted.

"Hang tight. Help's on the way."

Unceremoniously, St. Pierre reached between Bill and the passenger and pulled her up by the hand. "She is not hurt."

"She" was no girl. Her silhouette went in and out, not straight up and down. Beneath thick dark brows, her brown eyes projected terror, but she wasn't bleeding and everything looked like it worked. The only visible evidence that she'd just crashed into a wedding was the grass staining the tip of her longish nose and the yellow rose petals stuck to her dress.

The dog ran a joyful circle around her. St. Pierre slung an arm across her shoulders.

"Sauvignon? Chardonnay? Merlot?"

Savvy and her sisters stared, stupefied.

Behind them, all was silent. Everyone wanted to be able to say later that they heard the first words out of Xavier St. Pierre's mouth after he crash-landed smack into his eldest daughter's wedding.

"I present to you your half-sister, Sake."

Love the Napa Wine heiresses?

Be sure to check out the full series

Available now from Lyrical Press

HEATHER HEYFORD

A Taste of Chardonnay

THE NAPA WINE HEIRESSES

A TASTE OF CHARDONNAY

"Are you my Realtor?"

Chardonnay St. Pierre tried to hide her wariness as she approached the man who'd just stepped out of his retro pickup truck. This wasn't the best section of Napa city.

Their vehicles sat skewed at odd angles in the lot of the concrete building with the AVAILABLE banner sagging along one side. Around the back, gorse and thistles grew waist-high through the cracks in the pavement.

A startlingly white grin spread below the man's aviators.

"Realtor? You waiting for one?"

For the past half hour. "He's late." Char went up on her tiptoes, craning her neck to peer down the street for the tenth time, but the avenue was still empty. She tsked under her breath. She should've taken time after her run to change out of her skimpy running shorts, she thought, reaching discreetly around to give the hems a yank down over her butt. And her Mercedes looked more than a little conspicuous in this neighborhood.

Where was he? She pulled her cell out of her bag to call the Realtor back. But something about the imposing stranger was distracting her, demanding another look. "Have we met?" She squinted, lowering her own shades an inch.

He turned sideways without answering and examined the nondescript building, and when he did, his profile gave him dead away.

Oh my god. Char's breath caught, but he didn't notice. His whole focus was on the real estate. She'd just seen that face smiling out from the *People* magazine at the market over on Solano when she'd picked up some last-minute items for tonight's party.

"What have you got planned for the place?" he asked, totally unself-consciously.

Then she recovered. To the rest of the world, he was Hollywood's latest It Man. But to Char, he was just another actor. Who happened to have a really great dentist.

"I could ask you the same thing."

"I asked first."

Though she wasn't at all fond of actors, her shoulders relaxed a little. Obviously, she wasn't going to get raped out here in broad daylight by the star of *First Responder*. It was still in theaters, for heaven's sake. He couldn't afford the press.

Still. This building was perfect. And it'd been sitting here empty for the past three years. Just her luck that another party would be interested, right when Char was finally in a position to inquire about it.

To Char's relief, a compact car with a real estate logo plastered from headlights to tailpipe pulled up and a guy in his early thirties bounded out with an abundance of nervous energy.

"This business is *insane*," he said by way of introduction. "Dude calls me from a drive-by and wants me to show it to him, like, *now*, right? So I drop everything, even though I'm swamped with this new development all the way over on Industrial Drive. And then he doesn't show up till quarter of—"

He caught himself, pasted on a proper smile, and extended his hand toward It Man.

"Bill Diamond. And you're Mister . . . ?"

"McBride." The actor shook his hand, then turned and sauntered back to the building with his hands on his hips and his eyes scrutinizing its roofline.

"Ryder McBride?" asked Diamond. "*The* Ryder McBride? Oh!" A smile overspread his face. "Cool! Very cool. Nice to meet you, man." He nodded once for emphasis.

Char stepped up, removing her sunglasses and slipping them over the deep V of her racer-back tee.

"Hi." She thrust out her arm. "I'm—"

The Realtor's eyes grew even wider, as his hand reached for hers. "I know who you are . . . . *Chardonnay St. Pierre*."

He was still holding on when Char's phone vibrated in her other palm. One glance at the screen and she sighed.

"Excuse me."

But Diamond didn't let go.

"I've got to take this," she repeated, pronouncing each syllable slow and clear. She gave a little tug, and he came to, his fingers relaxing. "It's my little sister."

She ducked her chin and pressed answer.

"Where are you?" Meri's voice sounded tense.

"Downtown."

"You've got to come meet Savvy and me. Papa's in jail."

Bill Diamond was still gaping when Char dropped her phone into her shoulder bag.

"I'm so sorry. Something important's come up and I have to run."

Like a guy who'd come to expect disappointment at every turn, his face fell. "Oh."

Char felt a stab of empathy.

"Did you want to reschedule?" His brows shot up hopefully.

It was a given. But right now concern for her family eclipsed everything else. "I'll have to call you."

As she turned to go, Ryder spoke up.

"I'm staying. Mind showing me around?"

Char stopped in her tracks halfway to her car and glared back at him. She thought he'd barely noticed her. But she'd swear his broad grin was designed purely to tease.

"Excuse me? This is *my* Realtor."

"Ah, actually . . ." Bill cleared his throat, looked at the ground, and then back up at her. "I work for the seller."

"But *I'm* the one who called you to meet me here," she insisted.

He looked from Char to Ryder and back as he juggled his options, then shrugged. "But you're leaving."

Char's thoughts raced. She hated to leave those two here together, to cook up some deal to steal the building out from under her, but she had no choice. "Fine. Bill, I'll be in touch," she called, climbing into her car, then pulling out of the lot a little too fast.

She loved Papa. Truly, she did. But at times like these, she'd give anything for an ordinary, run-of-the-mill dad, in place of the notorious Xavier St. Pierre.

HEATHER HEYFORD

A Taste of Merlot

THE NAPA WINE HEIRESSES

A TASTE OF MERLOT

Grinning so hard her cheeks might burst, Merlot St. Pierre wove through the tightly packed crowd to the front of the art gallery, the jingling of her trademark stack of bracelets obscured by polite applause.

When she finally reached the podium, she clutched its clear acrylic edges and paused to commit the scene to memory, her gaze bouncing from face to familiar face. A rare sense of belonging washed over her, satisfying—if only for the moment—a cavernous emptiness inside.

Chardonnay and Sauvignon had even driven down from Napa for the annual exhibit—though not Papa, of course. He was perpetually busy, tied up in the never-ending cycle of planting, picking, and pressing grapes. Savvy smiled maternally, and Char brushed away a proud tear. Though they tried to blend in by hugging the wall at the back of the room, her sisters' expensive clothes and skyscraper heels elevated them to another class altogether. From a casual glance, nobody would've tagged Meri, in her scuffed flats and faded jeans, as their sister.

Just as well.

Meri waited for the clapping to taper off, then leaned into the mic. "To the Gates faculty, thank you from the bottom of my heart for this award. And to my fellow students, our shared appreciation for the craft I hope to spend the rest of my life perfecting fuses us together like one big, extended family."

The kind Meri had always wanted.

And in less time than it had taken to walk to the podium, her speech—and with it, the reception—was over.

Ten minutes later, still basking in the glow of her achievement, Meri excused herself from a small circle of well-wishers for a quick trip to the ladies' room. Hidden behind the stall door, she heard footsteps, followed by a voice.

"Did you see her up there?"

Meri's hand froze at the lock. She knew who that was. Her portfolio storage slot adjoined Meri's. They came in contact almost daily.

"The wine princess? I know. Made me want to gag. But you know how it is: 'Them that has, gets.'" *Chelsey.* Meri had known her since freshman year. "Still, it's not fair! She doesn't need the accolades. The rest of us are going to have to eke out a living, for real. How does *she* get the Purchase Prize?"

With shocked dismay, Meri flattened her palms against the door, cocked an ear, and held her breath, straining to hear through the sound of water running in the sink and paper towels being ripped from the dispenser. That first voice belonged to Rainn—like Meri, a jewelry major, except that she was a graduating senior and Meri still had another year to go.

"How do you think? Her old man donated a gazillion bucks to the college."

"Hmph," came another, mocking snort. "Should've guessed."

"Art is her hobby," said Rainn. It was the ultimate insider insult. "Everybody knows she'll never be a real jeweler. Just go back to Daddy's mansion and become a professional shopper."

"Have you seen it?" Chelsey asked.

"The winery? Only in pictures."

"She invited me up one time, over winter break. The pictures don't do it justice. Even if she does keep making jewelry after graduation, she'll never have to make a living at it. It's not fair. She's taking up space here that could've been given to a real artist. No wonder she calls her line 'Gilty.'"

Derisive laughter rang off the lavatory tiles. Still hidden, Meri cringed and squeezed her eyes closed, desperate for it to be over.

"C'mon, you look fine. It's the last Thirsty Thursday at O'Brien's. Everyone'll be there."

Everyone? Meri had spent last Thursday night hunched over her bench hook, buffing her final project. She'd been invited to O'Brien's once—back in the fall, after her twenty-first birthday—about the same time she'd developed a fascination with the historical uses of gemstones. She'd declined the offer in order to do research. She'd never been invited again.

A door creaked, and blessedly, the voices receded.

In a fog, Meri sank slowly onto the toilet seat and stared down at her cracked, work-stained fingertips until they all blurred together in her tears.

It was Mark Newman's idea to troll end-of-year student shows for fresh blood. While his boss at Harrington's was at least willing to humor him, if she'd had her druthers he'd be sticking with the stale, tried-and-true vendors.

After finding a parking spot, he walked all the way across the Gates College of Art and Design campus, only to find he was at the wrong building and had to cut back. He'd probably miss the speeches, but that was of no consequence. Receptions were for friends, family, and colleagues. Mark was there solely to see the work.

He'd scouted art schools in Chicago, Miami, and New York that spring, and so far, nothing had grabbed him. Where was all the new talent? Maybe Gloria was right, these excursions weren't worth the trouble.

He browsed through the two-dimensional art, the video installations, the ceramics and sculpture, saving the best for last. A leisurely, methodical sweep of the gallery was his way of pinpointing the location of the jewelry display cases, and as usual, he made a game out of it, letting the anticipation build, deciding which case he'd examine first and which he'd save for last.

When he finally got to the fixture in the center of the room, his roving eye came to an abrupt halt at five strands of flat braid connected by a perpendicular clasp. The alternating metals—yellow, white, and rose gold—lent fresh appeal to the simple design. Next to it, a royal-blue card with the words PURCHASE PRIZE sat slightly askew, a last-minute addition to the carefully arranged display. The piece begged to be touched, stroked—always a sign of good art. No wonder Gates had elected to buy it for its permanent collection over all the other projects created that year.

Mark looked up, his enthusiasm building by the second. Only a few people remained in the gallery, congregating quietly on the opposite side of the room. Deftly, he tried slipping his fingers into the crack between the lid and the side of the case. Locked, of course. Pulling out his jeweler's magnifying loupe, he bent close, straining to examine the piece as best he could through the layer of glass, to read the name on the hand-drawn tag attached by a silken cord.

GILTY. That was aggravating. He wanted a *real* name. On the other hand, the craftsmanship was *outstanding*. He'd never get over what could be achieved with simple tools in talented hands. Retail was his business, but design was his passion. Design, food, and football, in that order.

He let his loupe fall from the black leather thong around his neck and draped his hands possessively around the corners of the wide case, pulse quickening with the thrill of discovery. There had to be someone in authority here, someone with a key.

The reception was really winding down now; there was a growing trickle toward the exit. Mark didn't see anyone wearing a name tag. He went up behind two women who might be students.

"Excuse me." His voice sounded surprisingly calm, given how hard his heart thrummed. "Quick question."

The young women half-turned, their blank faces sizing him up with mild annoyance. Simultaneously, their eyes widened as they turned fully and broke out in cat-like smiles.

"Anything," the shorter, sultry-looking one purred, giving Mark a glimpse of the shiny barbell puncturing the center of her tongue.

Down, girl. Damn. He'd have to wear this old shirt more often.

"There's a mixed-metal bracelet over there with a tag that says 'Gilty.' The Purchase Prize winner. Know whose work it is?"

Their smiles went sour. The one with blue hair and a sleeve tattoo opened her mouth to speak but was interrupted by Barbell Girl.

"No idea," she interjected, eyeing Mark's loupe. "But hey, do you have a card or something? I can ask around. . . ."

"I'd appreciate it," he said, reaching into his back pocket.

"I'm Rainn, and this is Chelsey." Rainn lowered her lids while she drew a lengthy lock of raven-colored hair through stubby fingers, then tossed it back.

"Mark Newman." He peeled off a few cards and held them out.

"Harrington's?" Her smile morphed from merely seductive to blatantly opportunistic, displaying beautiful, white teeth. Individually they were perfect little pearls, but strung together they formed a wolfish grin that was downright unsettling.

"Nice meeting you. If you run into Gilty, have her—or him—give me a call."

He returned to the case, snapped some photos through the glass, and left the building.

He'd already forgotten the two students when he noticed them again across the street from the gallery, heads still bowed over his card like it was the key to the Grail.

He couldn't help smiling to himself. For an aspiring jeweler, *it was*.

As he walked back to his car, he pulled out his phone and scrolled for Gilty online, but nothing showed up.

So he'd call the school, first thing tomorrow morning.

He brightened with anticipation. Purchase Prize? He'd show them a purchase prize.

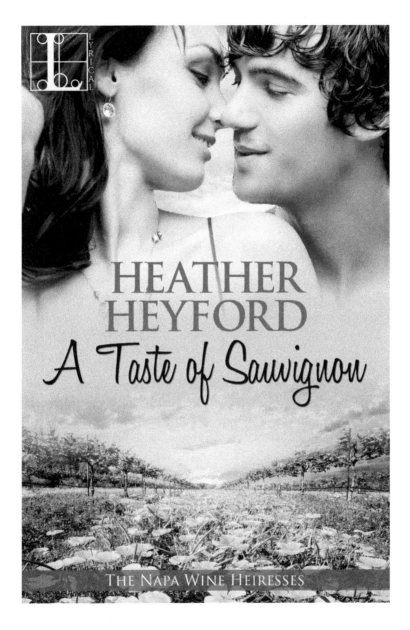

HEATHER
HEYFORD

A Taste of Sauvignon

THE NAPA WINE HEIRESSES

A TASTE OF SAUVIGNON

Sauvignon St. Pierre pulled the first little black dress from the left side of the rod in her precision-tuned walk-in closet. Later that evening, she would replace it on its padded hanger and hang it to the far right. And so on for the next two months, until today's dress came back into rotation.

From neat rows of acrylic boxes, each with a photo of its contents taped onto the end, she picked out a pair of two-and-a-half-inch black pumps.

The only aspect of her workday routine that couldn't be pre-arranged was which of her myriad fragrances to wear. Not even *she* could plan her mood ahead of time.

This morning, her hand hovered over flagons of every shape and pastel hue before landing on Maman's special rose perfume . . . for luck.

Savvy had made a calculated decision to become a lawyer when she was only thirteen. Fourteen years, three hundred thousand dollars in tuition, and two progressively thicker lenses later, she'd been offered a junior position with a small firm in her Napa hometown—either *because* her last name was St. Pierre, or in spite of it. And today, at the weekly meeting, she was finally being assigned her own case.

At precisely eight-thirty-five, one porcelain cup of chamomile tea, one bowl of Greek yogurt, and half a banana later, she slid into her black Mercedes to make it to her law office in time for the crucial nine o'clock meeting.

She looked both ways before steering the sleek sedan out of the long gravel drive of Domaine St. Pierre onto Dry Creek Road. Her car cut a perpendicular path between rows of yellow-green mustard flower buds alternating with what appeared to be dead sticks wedged upright in the soil. It was only March, though. The sap was rising. By summer, the mustard would be over and those "sticks," laden with leaves and berries, would steal the show, drawing thousands upon thousands of tourists to Napa Valley—doubling her drive time to and from work. But this morning, there was no other vehicle in sight.

She double-checked her reflection in the rearview to make sure the gold clasp on her pearls lay on her collarbone, just so. Then she pinched an earlobe to secure a diamond ear stud, brushed a microscopic speck of lint from her shoulder and cupped the chignon at the base of her neck.

Satisfied that all was in order, she began a mental preview of the day. She fast-forwarded, picturing herself seated side by side with the firm's partners around the long conference table, eager for the chance to finally prove herself worthy of someday becoming the first female partner at Witmer, Robinson and Scott.

"Diana! Susanna! *¡Vuelve!* Come back!"

Esteban leaned on the handle of his pitchfork, grinning as he watched his mother toddle after a clutch of her errant Ameracaunas. Expertly, she snatched up a hen into the crook of her arm and brandished a threatening finger in her face. *"¡Chica traviesa!* You naughty girl. How many times do I have to tell you do not go down the lane, eh?" Beneath her long strokes, the chicken's feathers flickered iridescent gold, green, and orange in the morning light. She softened her tone to a tender purr. "My beautiful little *chica.*"

Esteban shook his head. Madre was as fond of those stupid birds as she was of him and his sister. If possible, her attachment to her "girls" seemed to have only deepened, now that Esmerelda was married and living in Santa Rosa.

"Esteban! Can you look at the fence again? My *chicas* must have poked another hole somewhere," his mother pleaded, gently setting Marlena down with the others to shoo them back toward the paddock.

"Sí, Madre," he said, lapsing briefly into his native tongue.

Away from the farm, Esteban prided himself on his command of English. Mr. Bloomquist at Vintage High had even offered to write him a college recommendation.

"Your chem teacher said she'd write one, too," he'd coaxed. "We agree it would be a waste of your verbal and analytical skills not to continue your education. You could start out at NVCC and transfer to a four-year school later. . . ."

Esteban had been helping out on the family farm ever since he could lift a spade, but he'd never questioned why it was that plants were green. When he'd learned that what made them that way was a substance called chlorophyll that captured the sun's energy to make sugar out of air and water, he'd been fascinated. From then on, he'd been somewhat of a science geek.

After Mr. Bloomquist's offer, he'd imagined himself for a minute in a white lab coat, peering through a microscope at chloroplasts and ribosomes. The thought had made his scalp tingle.

But Esteban Morales was born to be a farmer. What would Padre do without him?

"This afternoon," he responded to Madre. First he needed to check on the effect of last night's rain on his tender lavender plants. The worst thing for lavender was mold.

Another stray—Natalia?—ran helter-skelter into Esteban's field of vision, down the muddy lane from where Padre had already thinned celery seedlings in the truck gardens earlier in the morning, past the paddock and the house toward Dry Creek Road. *¡Mierda!* Was he actually beginning to distinguish one of the flighty creatures from another?

"No this afternoon—now!" Madre scolded. She grabbed her broom from the porch and used it to sweep Natalia back toward the paddock. "You see this?" She gestured animatedly. "Before they all run onto the road and get hit by a car, and I have no chickens, no eggs, no money to pay the bills!"

Esteban chuckled under his breath. The Morales family would never be rich, yet they were hardly in dire straits. Losing a random eight-dollar chicken here and there wouldn't break the bank.

"Okay, okay."

Madre's appreciative grin was a reminder of her unconditional love, no matter how stern she pretended to be.

He continued in the direction of the shed. "I'll go get my tools."

Seconds later, he cringed at the squeal of rubber on asphalt and a sickening, avian screech.

Savvy slammed on the brakes the moment the chicken darted into view, but too late. She felt a thump, heard a squawk, and cringed. *I can't be late for work! Not today!* Yet something about the stricken expression on the face of the farm woman toddling toward her stabbed at her heart.

Mrs. Morales. She'd seen her stout silhouette a hundred times from a distance as she drove past the modest ranch house on Dry Creek Road, but she'd never met her next-door neighbor face-to-face. Still, thanks to Jeanne, the St. Pierre cook, she knew all about the Moraleses. Jeanne bought vegetables from their stand at the Napa farmers market. As far back as grade school, Jeanne had been rattling on about the Moraleses, their daughter, Esmerelda, and son, what's-his-name. But while Jeanne had only good things to say about the family, Papa always said Mr. Morales was nothing but a big pain in the *derriere*.

Savvy threw the gearshift into park, got out, and strode around to the right front tire, bracing for what she might find.

Directly behind the front passenger-side tire lay the deceased— intact, thankfully, but motionless, its beak frozen open in its final squawk.

"Marlena!" The older woman stopped short at the edge of the lane. Her chest heaved with effort. Calloused palms flung in help-lessness toward the dead animal. "*Marlena!*" she sobbed.

Savvy looked from Mrs. Morales's furrowed brow to the chicken—er, Marlena —and back.

Lips pressed into a tight line, she swallowed her squeamishness, squatting down for a better look. The last time she'd been this close to a chicken it had been covered in a delicate morel sauce.

What was she supposed to do? She glanced back up at Mrs. Morales to see her cross herself, then back down at Marlena. *Don't birds carry all kinds of diseases? Bird flu? Salmonella? Mites?*

She took a resigned breath, the farm odors of wet earth mingled with manure assaulting her senses, and steeled herself. This was all her fault. It was her responsibility to fix it.

Gingerly, she slid her bare hands under the hen's body. The unfa-miliar feel of stiff feathers atop warm jelly—apparently Marlena had been neither smart nor athletic—brought up the taste of bile. Some-how she found the strength to swallow it back.

Slowly, she turned and gently deposited the animal into its owner's outstretched arms.

"*Dios mío.*" Mrs. Morales hugged the hen to a bosom that threat-ened to ooze from between the buttons of her shirt and rocked the bird, all the while chanting something that sounded like, *sana, sana, colita de rana*—whatever that meant. Obviously, the chicken had been a well-loved pet.

"I'm so sorry!" Savvy cried, torn between the urge to embrace the grieving woman and the longing for a hazmat shower.

And then from out of nowhere, an agrilicious, king-sized man in faded jeans, snug plaid shirt, and silver belt buckle the size of a turkey platter jogged up to them, and in a flash, Savvy forgot all about death and God and germs. She even forgot about work.

Heather Heyford learned to walk and talk in Texas, then moved to England. *("Y'all want some scones?")* While in Europe, Heather was forced by her cruel parents to spend Saturdays in the leopard-print vinyl back seat of their Peugeot, motoring from one medieval pile to the next for the lame purpose of "learning something." What she soon learned was how to allay the boredom by stashing a *Cosmo* under the seat. Now a recovering teacher, Heather writes romance, feeds hard-boiled eggs to suburban foxes, and makes art in the Mid-Atlantic. She is represented by the Nancy Yost Literary Agency.